DICKSLIP

(A SCANDALOUS SLIP STORY #1)

GWYN MCNAMEE

DICKSLIP
Gwyn McNamee

All rights reserved. Except as permitted by U.S. Copyright Act of 1976, no part of this publication may be reproduced, distributed, or transmitted in any form or by any means, or stored in a database or retrieval system, without prior permission of the author. The scanning, uploading, and distribution of this book via the Internet or via other means without the permission of the publisher is illegal and punishable by law. Please purchase only authorized electronic editions and do not participate in or encourage electronic piracy of copyrighted materials. This book is a work of fiction. Names, characters, establishments, or organizations, and incidents are either products of the author's imagination or are used fictitiously to give a sense of authenticity. Any resemblance to actual persons, living or dead, events, or locales is entirely coincidental.

❦ Created with Vellum

BLURB

One wardrobe malfunction. Two lives forever changed.
Playing in a star-studded charity basketball game should be fun, and it is, until I literally go balls out to show up my arch nemesis. When I dive for the basketball and my junk slips out of my gym shorts, I know my life and career are over. There's no way the network can keep my kids' show on the air after I've exposed myself to millions of people. I don't know how Andy, the new CEO, can go to bat for me with such passion. I also never anticipate how hot she looks in a pair of high heels.

Rafe's dickslip has made my new job even more stressful. It's hard enough being a woman in a man's world without dealing with sex organs being publicly displayed when someone is representing the company. But he's an asset to the network, not to mention hot as hell. I can barely keep my eyes off him or his crotch during our meetings. Defending him to the board puts my ass on the line as much as his, but it's worth it. So is risking my job to fulfill the fantasies I've had about him since he first set foot in my office.

Things may have started out bad, but...
Some accidents have happy endings.

1

"Oh fuck."

I dive for the ball before it flies out of bounds.

The moment I land on the hard wood of the court, I know I've made a terrible mistake.

Shit.

It's not because of the pain radiating through my arm from the way I landed. That will go away.

But I almost wish I had broken something; it would be preferable to my current predicament. Because lying here on the side of the court with my dick hanging out the bottom of my bunched up shorts is basically the end my life as I know it.

It's just a damn charity game, but my need to show up Munro drove me to lunge after the ball like it was the NBA playoffs.

I should have just let it go, let it bounce off into the crowd of kids and their parents. But no, I had to go all NBA All-star and dive for it like my life depended on it...in my loose gym shorts and no jock strap.

The cool air of the arena on my dick and balls snaps me

to action, and I reach down and readjust as fast as I can. But it's too late.

Far, far too late.

The gasps rolling through the audience from parents and children alike are the death kiss to my career as a children's show host. I teach kids about dinosaur bones, not show them boners.

Not that I have one, but I might as well have a raging hard-on the way the parents are looking at me like I'm a pervert and covering the eyes of their kids with large hands.

Wide eyes and gaping mouths—that's all I see from the 15,000 plus spectators who came here to enjoy a basketball game played by celebrities.

This was definitely not what they paid for.

Holy shit.

I scrub my hands over my sweat-dampened face and will myself to wake up from this terrible nightmare.

This cannot be happening.

Not now.

Why God? Why?

What the hell did I do to karma to make that bitch torture me like this?

I'm a good person...I think. I don't stab people in the back. I don't gossip. I donate to the church and do these charity events.

What did I do to deserve this clusterfuck in my life?

A hand extends over me, offering to assist me back to my feet. I almost take it until I shift my head to avoid the bright overhead lights and see who it's attached to.

Munro. That motherfucker.

If it weren't for him, none of this would have happened.

The asshole just can't accept that he's number two in the ratings for a reason. And I just had to stick it to him and rub it in his face on the court too. They put us on opposing teams for a reason, to cash in on the rivalry that already exists between us. And my team has been kicking ass all game. Until my epic dive into unemployment and internet meme fame.

Lord, did this just backfire on me.

I know he's going to milk this any way he can to try to move his show, *Bones and More*, up to the top of the ratings. And I'm sure he's devious enough to make it work. There's no way to avoid it. This asshole won't just let it go. It's not in his nature.

"Looks like you could use a..." his eyes flick down to where my cock sits nestled back in my shorts, "small hand."

Asshole.

I bat his proffered hand away and climb to my feet under my own steam. There's no way I'm letting this jerkoff touch me and look like the fucking hero coming to my rescue.

The crowd doesn't know whether to celebrate the fact that I'm uninjured or continue to react to my wardrobe malfunction. A sporadic, half-hearted clap accompanies murmurs and laughs.

Fucking A.

It's the worst thing to happen to clothes since that whole Super Bowl incident. But at least then, we all knew it was planned. Flashing my junk to the entire audience, as well as all those watching on TV, was most certainly not on the agenda when I signed up to play in this charity game for the children's hospital.

And instead of playing a friendly game of basketball and raising money for the sick kids, I just shot down my career with a scud missile.

Somehow, I force myself to ignore the gawking stares and whispered words and make my way to where the rest of the players wait for the ball to be inbounded. All that and I didn't even save the damn thing.

Jason Rodney slaps me on the back with a grin. "You good, buddy?"

I nod and try to avoid eye contact. If he mentions what just happened, I'll be even more mortified than I already am.

I'll never live this down. It will haunt me the rest of my life, and that's a long fucking time.

Jesus, Rafe, you really did it this time.

And it couldn't have come at a worse time for the show or the network. Andy Mason has only been CEO for twenty-four hours, and I've already gone and exposed my junk on national television.

Why did they have to show this thing live?

If this had been recorded and replayed, it may have saved me from the rest of the world seeing my cock and balls. At least it would have only been the people in here. But who am I kidding? Someone, no doubt, has it on a cell phone video anyway. There's no way this *wasn't* getting out, one way or the other.

I'm too busy berating myself to notice the ball flying at my face until it's too late.

Crack.

Blood gushes from my nose and down my white jersey as pain assaults my face.

Motherfucker!

Cries ring out from the crowd, and I fall to my knees on the court clutching my face. Through some immense self-control, I manage to refrain from cursing on national television, but the damage has been done.

I'm pretty sure my nose is broken along with my pride.

You have got to be fucking kidding me.

2

My heels clatter to the tile under my desk, and I wiggle my toes and then press my feet flat against the cool floor. It feels so good to be out of those things. I love my heels. But damn. The last twenty-four hours have left me reconsidering my stance on daily stilettos.

I take a look around my new office and try to just enjoy it for a minute. God knows I haven't had any time to in the last day since I took over. But that's good, I think. The board wants me to hit the ground running and I did, even in these killer heels. And I'm not about to slow down, except for now, for five damn seconds to catch my breath and stretch my cramped toes.

The fact that I have this job is still hard to grasp. The youngest CEO in KBC history and its first woman.

How the hell did this even happen?

Yes, I've busted my ass to get here, but the board must have passed over a hundred better qualified and more experienced applicants to get to me. I know I interviewed well, but the fact they put the future of this network in my hands still gives me goose bumps.

Years of climbing the corporate ladder in a good ol' boys business environment hasn't been easy. But I made it, even if my feet are killing me for it.

A smile spreads across my face, and I recline back in my chair and spin to face the wall of windows that overlooks L.A.

This city will eat you alive if you let it. But I won't. I'll be the best damn CEO this network ever had. Even if it means sore feet, no sleep, and no time for sex. Though that last one is a real bummer.

The last few months have been such a whirlwind, I've barely had a chance to break out my B.O.B. let alone find time to spend with a real man. Most nights, I drop into bed so exhausted, the only thing on my mind is sleep for as long as I can find it.

And let me tell you, that makes for a very lonely existence. I have Christian Louboutin, Jimmy Choo, and Sergio Rossi to keep me company. But they are sharp and don't keep the bed very warm at night. I'd much rather have someone to come home to. But finding someone who understands my work schedule and isn't intimidated by a woman in my position has been difficult, if not impossible.

Jeff only lasted four months before he told me "women aren't supposed to have more balls than a man," and took off for greener pastures. Lawrence didn't even last that long. I think it was only six weeks with him.

When did a strong woman knowing what she wants become a bad thing?

It seems the higher I advance in my career, the harder it becomes to maintain any semblance of an adult relationship. No strings attached sex is great, but one cannot live on bread (or sex) alone. And now that I have this job, things are only going to get harder.

A knock at the door breaks my reverie and I spin back toward my office, slightly perturbed. "Yes?"

Penny pops her head in and bites her lip. "I'm sorry to interrupt, ma'am."

I wave her in. As annoyed as I am to be interrupted, I know she wouldn't be coming in if it weren't important. She's been with me long enough to know when to leave me alone and when something can't wait. "It's fine. What do you need?"

She twists her hands together in front of her and shifts her weight. Penny came with me from the tiny MBC affiliate and she knows the business and me like the back of her hand, so seeing her this flustered sends acid churning in my gut.

This isn't going to be good.

"Well, um, something happened at the charity basketball game today that requires your attention."

I almost forgot about the game today. We had at least a dozen personalities from our shows playing, and it was simulcast on at least ten networks. I wish I could have watched it. There's nothing more entertaining than actors trying to play sports. Plus, I love a good ball game.

The clock on my computer reads 5:30. I want nothing more than to go home, slip into a pair of leggings, and open a large bottle of wine. "Can it wait until tomorrow?"

Penny pulls her lip between her teeth again and shakes her head. "I don't think so, ma'am."

I heave out a sigh and brace myself for what can only be bad news. "Well, what happened?"

She blushes ten shades of red and runs a shaky hand

over her skirt. "Uh, well...there was a wardrobe malfunction."

A wardrobe malfunction? What the hell does that mean? Someone's uniform ripped?

All I can picture is Janet Jackson's tit hanging out when I hear that term.

"What do you mean?"

She lets out a shaky, unsure laugh. "Well, Rafe Boswell dove for a ball, and well...his thing came out along with, well...you know...the other bits."

His *thing*?

Oh, HELL no!

Visions of FCC investigations and fines flit through my head. This is bad.

"You're kidding, right?"

Penny shakes her head. "I wish I were."

Fudge.

"At least tell me it wasn't caught on camera."

That lip disappears again before she responds, and I already know what's coming. "Unfortunately, it was broadcast on every station that was showing it live."

I try to suck back the urge to scream.

On my second day? For the love of all that's holy, why does it have to happen now?

"Holy hell. Get me a copy of that video immediately and schedule Rafe to come in first thing in the morning. He's probably going to be busy licking his wounds tonight."

Penny let's out an awkward chuckle. "Probably, since he also got hit in the face with a ball and broke his nose."

Facepalm.

I drop my face into my hand and sigh.

No. Double facepalm. This calls for two.

3

Sitting outside Andy Mason's office feels like waiting for my execution. My face still throbs from the broken nose, but at least I don't need surgery to fix it and the bruising hasn't started yet.

I can only imagine what I'm going to look like tomorrow. The last time I got punched in the face was college, and it wasn't pretty the next day. I'm lucky it's held off this long.

I wish I could've avoided this altogether and just turned in my resignation, but I'm not a total fucking pussy. I need to at least attempt to stand up for myself and argue to keep my job when Andy tries to can me.

It wasn't like it was my fault. I certainly never planned for this to happen.

They can't fire me for an accident, can they?
Who am I kidding? Of course they can.

Everything on television is about appearances, and right now, I'm *The Bone Doctor*, the friendly TV host who teaches kids about dinosaurs and skeletons and other fun, scientific things. If they don't fire me, it's only a matter of time before I'll be called The Boner Doctor or Dr. Boner or something equally terrible. I'm sure Munro has already started calling me any number of things in his circles.

I've avoided my phone and social media completely since I got home last night. I don't have the stomach for it right now. I'm sure Mom and Riley have called a hundred times, but I don't need my mother and my sister weighing in on this incident. I have more important worries than what they think about it.

This is bad for my image and the image of the network, so they have to fire me. They don't have a choice.

Seriously, one dive for a ball and this is where I find myself, waiting to be fired. So much for helping out a charity.

"Rafe?"

I glance up and see the new assistant, Penny, waiting for me at the end of the couch. "Andy will see you now."

Wonderful.

I push up to my feet and follow her to the large double doors that lead into the CEO's office. Andy's reputation precedes him. I've heard about what a fucking hardass he can be and how impossible it is to please him, so I can only imagine how this conversation will go.

Not fucking smoothly.

Penny throws open the doors, and I follow her in and stop in my tracks when a beautiful blonde rises from her chair behind the desk and walks over to me in long, elegant strides wearing heels high enough to almost put her on my eye level.

Her smile lights up her face and a faint pink blush covers her pale cheeks.

"Rafe, it's nice to meet you. I'm Andy Mason." She holds out her hand, and it takes me a moment to realize I'm supposed to shake it.

Fuck.

She must be an Andrea. It would've been nice if someone had mentioned that to me so I didn't come in here looking like a fucking idiot. I manage to stop drooling long enough to take her proffered hand and give it a shake and a squeeze. Her firm grip matches mine, and she smiles at me again, flashing bright, perfectly straight teeth.

A small hand points toward a chair. "Please, take a seat. Can Penny get you anything to drink?"

I clear my suddenly dry throat. "Uh, no. I'm fine, thank you." I lower myself into one of the high-back chairs that faces her desk, and the whole city of Los Angeles is sprawled out behind her.

"Beautiful office." *Lame, Rafe. Real fucking lame.*

But I can't think of anything else to say. The situation is pretty fucking awkward as it is, and finding out that she's not a man makes it ten times worse.

How do I talk to my female boss, my smoking hot female boss, about my dick coming out in the middle of a basketball game?

She leans her elbows on the desk and gives me a knowing smile before clasping her hands in front of her.

"Well Rafe, you know why I've called you here."

I shove my hand back through my hair and tug on the ends. "Yeah, I have some idea."

"Pretty embarrassing, wasn't it?" The corner of her mouth tilts up into a grin, and I can't help but smile back despite wanting to crawl under the desk and die.

"You could say that."

Humor and concern play in her green eyes. "First and foremost, let me ask, how is your nose?"

I instinctively reach up and press my finger against it then wince at the pain that shoots in my sinuses. "It's okay.

They reset it and said I don't need to have surgery or anything. It should heal in a couple weeks."

She nods and offers a soft smile. "Well, obviously, you won't be filming during that time because I assume you're going to start getting some pretty nasty bruises around the eyes."

"Filming?" I jerk my head back up to look at her. I must have heard her wrong.

"Of course. You are in the middle of filming your new season, aren't you?"

"Yeah, but I just assumed—"

She holds up a hand to stop me. "You assumed you were going to be getting fired when I called you in here."

Ding. Ding. Ding.

"Well, yeah, I mean, it seems like a pretty logical assumption."

She laughs and the light tinkling sound hardens my cock unexpectedly.

Damn, she's fucking gorgeous, especially when she laughs. I'm thankful this giant desk separates us so she can't see this massive hard-on I'm sporting.

"Well, the second thing I was going to tell you is that you're not fired. It was an accident, anybody can see that. As far as I'm concerned, we will make a statement to the press and then let it be done and over with. No one in their right mind believes that you intentionally did that."

If only that were enough.

"It's not about whether it was intended or not. People saw it; it was all over the airwaves."

She nods and gives me another soft smile, her compassion over the situation evident. "Yes, that's true, but you have a stellar reputation in the business, and you are our number one show in the kids' categories. I'm not about to cancel it and leave that spot open so that Munro can sweep in and steal it."

Well, I'll be damned. Smart as a fucking whip, this one.

"I see you know about him."

This time, her smile has a hard edge to it. "It's hard not to. The guy has been gunning for you since the show came on the air. He basically stole your platform."

"Don't I know it." Munro's show, *Bones and More,* aired on a rival network a mere month after *The Bone Doctor* premiered. I have no doubt in my mind somebody from our team leaked the plans for the show and they just rushed to try to get to market before we did.

They're trying to jump on the same bandwagon we were with the revival of the Jurassic Park series. Interest in dinosaurs and other archaeological things has skyrocketed again, and this seemed like a great way to get in on it. I was basically poached from the Natural History Museum to act as host. They said I was a natural in front of the camera with my good looks and paleontology background.

I was perfect for it.

And they were right; my show was an instant hit and has held the top of the rankings for the last two years. Even though Munro has been breathing down my neck, he hasn't been able to knock me out of that spot. The fact that Andy has this much confidence in me makes me feel marginally better than I did last night when I went home and drank a fifth of whiskey.

"You really think a statement is going to be enough?"

She holds her hands up and shrugs. "I don't know. All we can do is try. I'm meeting with the board tomorrow, and I'm going to argue your case. You get a couple weeks off anyway so just sit tight and try not to worry about it too much. I mean, a wardrobe malfunction is a wardrobe function. It's not the end of the world, just a little cock and balls."

Her hands shoot up over her mouth as soon as the words are out of it, and her eyes widen. "Shit. I didn't mean to say that out loud. Please don't sue me for sexual harassment."

I laugh and wave my hands in the air to indicate it was nothing.

I can't believe she just said that, but her reaction is incredibly endearing. "Don't worry, I get it."

Although, she did say *little* and that irks me more than I'd like to admit. I've never been embarrassed about the size of my dick, but now two comments in two days? It's starting to hurt my already bruised ego a bit.

Andy pushes to her feet and smooths down the green dress she's wearing before walking around to my side of the desk. It clings to all her curves like she was poured into it. It should be a sin to look that good in a dress, especially in a business setting. I rise too, careful to discreetly adjust my raging cock so it's not springing out in her direction.

"Well, on that note, thank you for coming, Rafe. I appreciate you speaking with me."

I take her hand again, and our palms linger against each other longer than is probably appropriate. Sparks shoot up my arm, and my cock throbs again.

Jesus, who would've thought Andy Mason would be a woman and a sexy one at that.

Sexy and formidable.

She has me almost believing my job is as safe as she says it is.

4

"You can't be serious, Andrea."

The six men sitting around the conference room table all stare at me like I'm some creature from another planet. I'm used to being gawked at in this business. But the slackjaws looking back at me now are something totally unexpected given our topic of conversation.

How can they not understand where I'm coming from on this?

They're men, one would think this may have happened to them at some point in their own lives and they'd have some sympathy. But since the moment I set foot in this board meeting, it's been nothing but "fire him, fire him, fire him" coming from their old, crusty, geriatric mouths.

"I am serious, gentlemen. Rafe is a tremendous asset to this network, and I'm not willing to let an accident derail what both he and my predecessor worked so hard to build."

Barry sighs and takes a sip of his coffee. The man is a legend in this industry and has led the board for the last quarter century. Still, that doesn't mean I have to like what he has to say or agree with him.

"I appreciate your passion, Andy. It's why we hired you over all the other applicants, but this was more than a little accident. His genitals were on full display. Now we are dealing with the FCC and an investigation, not to mention the public reaction. Have you seen the internet today?"

Unfortunately, I have.

Every celebrity gossip site on the web seems to have latched on to this story and run with it. Still images and videos of Rafe's junk are plastered all over for anyone to see. And even though it's wrong...really, really burn in Hell kind of wrong...I've looked...more than once.

I wish I could say it was for business reasons, to gauge how bad the situation really is, but it's not. I'm just a big ol' perv who is enjoying staring at a beautiful cock. Because make no mistake, Rafe has a gorgeous one. And if I weren't his boss, I would want to help him lick his wounds...and something else.

I've been far too busy worrying and planning for this new job to spend any time looking for someone to spend my time with. And Rafe is exactly the kind of man I'm normally attracted to—tall, dark, and handsome. Plus, he's brilliant. It's a lethal combination to my libido. I've seen him on the small screen a hundred times, but when he walked into my office yesterday, swollen nose and all, I was instantly aware that the camera cannot capture everything. The man oozes sex appeal and is charming as hell even when he's floundering and worried. I wanted to take him in my arms and tell him everything would be okay, and then bang him on my desk.

Yeah, being the boss sucks sometimes, because that can never happen. Nothing ever can.

I clear my throat and stare Barry down. "I've seen it, and I don't care. Everyone knows it was an accident, and calling him 'Dr. Boner' isn't going deflect from the fact that he's number one in the ratings. We don't often find a man with a background as stellar as Rafe's who is so incredible on camera. Kids love him, and I'm not willing to throw that away over this."

A collective round of sighs fills the room, and Barry scans the faces of the other board members before settling on mine again. "This is only your third day on the job. Are you really willing to risk it over Rafe Boswell?"

Am I?

The man is fantastic at what he does. I've never seen such a natural on camera who's so good with kids and who can explain scientific things that should be way over their heads in such an accessible way. He really is an asset to this network. I'm not just blowing smoke because I think he's hot. But it probably would be a lot easier just to fire him and get this over with. He can be replaced, probably not by someone who is as good as he is, but everyone is replaceable in this industry.

It would mean losing the top spot to Munro, which would be like kicking me in the balls, but maybe it is taking on too much to do this.

Just as I'm reconsidering the stance I've taken, I take a good look at the old men shifting around the table, and I realize that's exactly what they want. They may have hired me, but no man from this generation really wants a woman in charge. They think *they* still run this show. They want me to back down. They want me to give in, and I'm not going to let them have that satisfaction.

"Yes, I'm sure. Rafe Boswell stays. I've already prepared a statement for the press today, and as soon as that's done, he has a couple weeks off to recover and then we go back to filming. We will not acknowledge any questions or comments about the incident. As far as I'm concerned, it's in the past and it's going to stay that way. This is my network now, and I plan on doing everything I can to keep it profitable, and that means keeping Rafe Boswell here as long as we can. I'm not going to let some stupid incident scare me away from that. And neither should you."

All sets of eyes are on me as I finish my rant. I hadn't intended to come off so bitchy, but frankly, the fact that they don't trust me to make this decision irks me.

I know I just started and I haven't proven myself, but I would think my track record would be enough. It got me this job. But they are already questioning my first big decision. I understand their concerns, but they need to put their trust in me to handle this situation and know what I'm doing.

Now, I have something to prove, and that means my life is now in the hands of Rafe Boswell.

5

I stare at my phone and go over the message in my head. Andy wants to meet with me again. Her message said we needed to talk before the press statement.

She met with the board today.

My hand shakes slightly as I delete the message, and my eyes travel over the hundred or so messages I've ignored over the last few days. I won't be able to put off Riley or Mom much longer. The rest of my friends, maybe, but not family. I've only spoken with a few friends, those I *thought* would be understanding and supportive. Boy, was I wrong. I'm the laughing stock of L.A. Even my own friends can't help themselves from cracking jokes at my expense.

I can't deal with more of that right now. Not when my job is on the line.

Assholes.

The board has the final word on everything at the network. Andy may be in charge, but they're the ones who put her in that position. They can overrule her if they really want to, which means I may be going in to get canned... again. I would like to think she wouldn't drag it out and would just tell me, but that's not something you do in a message.

I return my phone to its charger and wander into the bathroom to get ready for the meeting. Almost as soon as I flip on the shower, steam begins to form on the mirror.

With a sigh, I swipe it away and examine myself to check out the damage to my face. Surprisingly, I haven't gotten black eyes or bruising at all from the broken nose, and the swelling has all but disappeared. I don't know what gods smiled upon me with that; they certainly haven't been involved in anything else that happened the last couple days.

If I get one more call from a friend or family member wanting to talk about what happened, I may move to the wilderness and become a lumberjack just to get away from it. Or at the very least, return to the bowels of the museum to work in peace and obscurity.

Yes, it happened.

Yes, it was embarrassing.

Yes, I want to crawl into the cave.

And no, I don't want to talk about it...ever.

If I have to repeat those words one more time, I don't think I can handle it. At least if I was filming or working, things would be a little bit better. I'd have something to occupy my mind, but instead, I'm just sitting here waiting for another two weeks before I'm back in front of the camera.

Maybe I can ask Andy to tell the producers that since it looks like I'm not going to bruise, we can resume taping right away. That is...if I still have a job.

The fact that she just met with the board and also wants to meet with me again does not sit well. Those old codgers are known for having sticks up their asses.

Having my dick on full display probably did not endear me to them.

I guess I'll find out after my shower.

The hot water does nothing to release the tension in my shoulders or my gut. And it's not just because I might lose my job; it's that woman.

She is sex on a stick. There's just something about a powerful woman who takes control and knows what she wants that does something to me, and Andy is precisely all those things.

The other day, she took command of the room the second I stepped in it and wasn't afraid to be direct until she thought I might sue her. I chuckle at the slip of her tongue.

Christ, the way she blushed was adorable.

The pink slowly spreading up her chest and over her neck and cheeks.

I want her to blush like that for me, because I'm between her legs and driving her insane. My cock hardens at the image. At least I didn't break *it* in this fiasco.

Taking my aching cock in my hand, I flatten the other against the tile wall of the shower and picture Andy. She's a force in the office, and I'm sure she's the same in the bedroom.

Licking and sucking my dick.

Swallowing me down.

It doesn't take long for my strokes to turn frantic, and when I come, jets shooting across the tile, I have to remind myself to breathe.

Holy hell, that woman can do that to me without even touching me.

If she were here for real, I wouldn't last two seconds. But at least it's out of my system for when I meet with her. There's nothing more embarrassing than walking into a meeting with your boss with a raging boner, except maybe having your junk broadcast on national television.

Been there. Done that.

I don't need any embarrassing repeats. The hard-on I got during our last meeting was incredibly inappropriate, and I don't need her seeing that and thinking I'm some sex-crazed pervert.

Even if she wanted it too, it can never happen between us anyway. She's off-limits. She's the boss. She's also intimidating as hell. She would probably swallow me whole after sex, like some sort of deranged praying mantis.

Why is that so fucking hot, though?

This scandal requires me to lay low for a while. Getting involved with the boss would be the opposite of that. Besides, I don't want her going to bat for me for the wrong reasons. The outcome would be both of our asses in a sling.

6

Why does he have to be so damn handsome?

The whole maintaining a professional demeanor thing would be a lot easier if my entire being wasn't screaming at me to flirt with Rafe.

He strides over to my desk with a hesitant smile.

Don't look at his dick. Don't look at his dick.

Crap. I failed miserably at that.

The way his pants hug his legs and crotch, it leaves little to the imagination. And I don't need imagination after replaying that damn video a thousand times.

He reaches my desk and extends his hand. I rise to greet him, and the moment our hands touch, a tidal wave of warmth floods my body. He feels it too. I know he does. The raised eyebrow and his lingering squeeze of my hand tells me I'm not the only one who's experiencing a physical reaction. And damn if that doesn't suck.

I haven't met a man I'm this into in years, and he has to be my employee. One who is already in hot water.

"Please take a seat, Rafe."

He unbuttons his perfectly tailored suit jacket and slowly lowers himself into one of the chairs facing my desk.

Don't look at his dick. Don't look at his dick.

My eyes drift of their own accord and I find myself staring at his lap, barely visible over the edge of the desk.

He clears his throat, refocusing my attention to his face. A grin slants his mouth. "I assume you want to discuss your meeting with the board and my statement for today?"

I nod and try not to drool over the way his jacket is pulling taut across his biceps when he shifts. "Yes. I thought we could go over everything."

"Fire away."

I chuckle at his choice of words that I'm sure was intentional. "You're not getting fired. The board may have concerns, but I'm the one calling the shots, and I say you stay."

His brow furrows, and he leans forward slightly. "Does that mean you're putting your own job at risk by standing up for me with the board?"

That's a hard one to answer and one I would rather avoid altogether. Rafe strikes me as the type to be heroic and throw himself on the sword to protect a woman. I can't see him being okay with what went down in that boardroom.

"If this goes south, it's your ass on the line." Barry's words ring in my ears as Rafe waits patiently for my response.

I clear my throat. "That isn't any of your concern. You do your job and I'll do mine."

Rafe considers me for a moment, his long fingers steepled over a luscious mouth I'd kill to kiss. "Andy, I appreciate what you're doing for me, but please don't risk your career for mine. I have other things I can do. It wouldn't be the end of the world."

Didn't I tell him not to worry about it?

Part of me wants to remind him who's in charge here, but the other part recognizes that he's only trying to do the right thing. I can't really blame him for that. He was probably raised right, to be chivalrous toward women and offer them assistance, even if they don't need it.

Don't be offended, Andy. Take it as a compliment he wants to protect you.

I smile and wring my hands together in front of me. "I'm not worried, Rafe. And you shouldn't be either, unless you've changed your mind and you're telling me you want to resign?"

A smirk overtakes his face, and he drops his hands onto his thighs.

Christ, I want to see what his legs look like under that black fabric. Probably thick and muscular...I'm sure the video didn't do him justice.

"No, I'm not quitting. I just realize that this situation may be more than is fixable, and I don't want to be responsible for you losing your job too."

My spine snaps straight, and I narrow my eyes on him. "I can assure you, Rafe, I am *responsible* for my own actions and how they affect *my* life."

He grins. "Oh, I have no doubt about that, Andy."

His words drip with sexual innuendo, and the air in the room thickens. The large space suddenly feels like a tiny coat closet with both of us crammed into it.

"Are you so eager to get back to the museum? Are you sick of the spotlight already?"

A laugh rumbles from his chest. "The last few days have certainly given me reason to second-guess my decision to leave the museum, but no, I'm not looking to go back there. I love doing this."

"Good. Then let's go over the statement I've prepared for

the press conference today. I've made a few changes since yesterday based on some comments from the board, but it's largely unchanged from what we previously discussed."

He nods and reaches out to take the proffered sheet of paper. "I trust that anything you've prepared is fine."

"I appreciate the confidence in my abilities, but you do have some say in this. If there's anything you aren't comfortable with, please let me know, and I can run any changes by legal before we go live."

His focus centers on the paper and that leaves me time to drink him in without being noticed.

Damn. This man really is something else.

His dark hair and olive complexion are enhanced by the dark black suit and blue shirt combination molded to his body—a body I have no doubt is toned and absolutely lickable from what little I saw on the video.

I almost wish he would quit to remove any impediment between us. But that's selfishness talking, not the shrewd business woman who knows what an asset he is to this network.

He finishes his perusal of the document and returns his dark bourbon eyes to me. "This looks good. Let's run with this."

"Great." I stand and move around to the end of the desk. "Then I'll see you in about an hour to head to the press conference. I'll escort you down and say a few words before I bring you on to speak."

Rafe rises from his chair and approaches me slowly, his eyes roaming over my black dress and red heels. "Do you think that's wise? Appearing on camera for something like this so early in your tenure? Why not let someone from legal or PR handle it?"

I narrow my eyes on him and lift my chin. "You don't

seem to be understanding, Rafe...this is my show. I'll do whatever I want."

He steps into me, far closer than is appropriate for the situation, and a tingle of excitement races through me. "Yes, it would seem you are firmly in control here, Andy."

7

The bright lights of the cameras shine into my eyes. I blink against them as I take my place on the small stage just to the right of the podium.

Andy brushes past me on her way to the microphone, and the swirl of her heady scent—some sort of flower, maybe Jasmine—invades my senses. I barely managed to contain the raging hard-on I had during our meeting and now it's threatening to make a reappearance.

She hasn't even uttered a single word, but she already commands the entire room. Everyone silences without being asked and sits at the ready waiting for her to speak. She turns and glances back at me only briefly before she dives in.

"Hello. My name is Andrea Mason. As most of you undoubtedly know, I am the new CEO of KBC network. While I may have only started a few days ago, already I've been forced to come forward as the official head of the network to make this statement on something I'd hoped I wouldn't have to. We all know what happened at the charity game. I won't rehash it, and I don't expect you to either."

The crowd remains silent and watches her rapt. I do the same. She's in complete control and everyone hangs on her every word. She could be listing off an ingredient list for banana bread and everyone would be absolutely enthralled with her. Or maybe that's just my libido talking.

Lord knows, this woman has me wound tighter than a spring, and I'm ready to snap. The stress of the last few days combined with the undeniable attraction between us is driving me slowly insane.

"Rafe Boswell has been a member of the KBC family for the past two years, and his show, *The Bone Doctor*, has remained at the number one spot in his category since essentially the day it premiered. Everyone knows Rafe, and we all know he is an upstanding and well-loved member of this community. The fact that I even have to make this statement or say anything is more irritating than I'd like to admit; however, there are people who would like to see Rafe's good name tarnished. And so, it becomes necessary for us to come forward today to make this brief statement. We will not be accepting any questions after."

She turns back toward me and holds her hand out. "Rafe."

I step forward into the spotlight. All eyes are trained on me as they await my statement. The few steps to the podium feel like a mile. Andy waits until I'm right next to her. She places a reassuring hand on my shoulder before she steps away.

The touch of her hand, even through the material of my shirt and jacket, sears my skin and also gives me the confidence to proceed with my statement when all eyes are on me.

You can do this.

Several deep breaths minimally help in slowing my

racing heart, but my chest still tightens looking out at the crowd of reporters.

Who would have thought so many people would care what I have to say?

They probably don't. They probably just want to see me go down in flames in person. Maybe they're hoping for a repeat performance. Maybe a split in my pants and a fall off the stage.

I shudder at the thought and take a deep breath again to try to regain my composure. I've never been afraid of public speaking before, but now, my palms are sweating, and I swear, the temperature jumped about twenty degrees the second I got behind the podium.

"Uh, hello. I'm Rafe Boswell." I glance down at the prepared statement and try to remember what I'm supposed to be saying. "The incident at the charity game was an unfortunate accident. I deeply regret any traumatic effects it may have had on any spectators or viewers. However, I also feel I must address the vicious rumors being spread. Any insinuation that what happened was in any way planned is absolutely ludicrous and false. I respect and cherish the trust parents and children put in me as the host of *The Bone Doctor*, and I would never abuse that trust as others are suggesting. I hope we can put this in the past and move forward without further dragging me through the mud. Thank you."

I added that last line myself. I probably should have left it alone and stuck with the prepared statement, but the fact that any media outlet thinks it's okay to run such a ridiculous story...that I would ever intentionally show my junk to thousands of people...just blows my mind. It has to stop.

Andy approaches and places her small hand on my

shoulder, ushering me away from the platform as questions are hurled at us from all directions.

She doesn't acknowledge them, just continues to lead me away from the stage and down the hallway toward the conference room.

We pause outside the door, and she finally removes her hand. She offers a small, apologetic smile. "You did well."

Then, she turns on her heels and elegantly walks down the long hallway back to her office without looking back, as if nothing happened.

8

Today was long. Epically long.

The only thing I wanted to do was grab a bite, a couple drinks, and then head home, kick off these heels, and drop into bed.

But it's turned into a binge night.

I'm on drink what…three? And I haven't even finished dinner yet. It was that meeting with Rafe and then the press conference. Just sitting across from him in my office was enough to get me hot and bothered.

That man gets under my skin in a way I never anticipated. It's one thing to be attracted to him, but this is far more than that. I was tempted to throw caution to the wind and act on it, ask him out, ask him to come back to my place…

Idiot.

You're his boss, Andy. You can't ask him out. You can't proposition him. You can't have him.

And that fucking blows.

So, yeah, on to drink number four.

I've earned it after this first week. There's no way it could have been any worse. Between Rafe's wardrobe malfunction and the stress of trying to establish myself as the head honcho in a man's world at a network that has never had a female CEO before, this is exactly what I need on a Friday night.

My regular bartender, Jared, is eyeing me with a grin from the other end of the bar, and if it weren't for my current Rafe obsession, I might consider bringing him home again. We had a fun time the last few times we hooked up. But I don't just want a hookup. I want Rafe.

The din of voices and music filling the bar mixed with the booze my brain is swimming in almost helps me forget my predicament. Almost.

These drinks are running through me. I need to take a bathroom break before I return to guzzling whiskey like it's water.

"Jared, I'll be right back." I point to my half-eaten plate of pasta and motion toward the back hallway where the bathrooms are located. He nods and gives me a smile.

I make my way toward the bathrooms, brushing past waiters and other patrons milling about waiting for their tables in the main restaurant area. This place is always packed, especially on a Friday night. But the food is amazing and the drinks are always served with a smile, so eating at the bar before heading home seemed like a great plan.

But stumbling down the dark hallway, I'm starting to think maybe drinking alone was a bad idea. My hand grips the wall for balance.

Damn these gorgeous heels.

I manage to get to the bathroom and take care of business unscathed, but on the return stumble down the hallway, my heel catches on something, partially pulling it from my foot, and I tumble forward into a hard, warm chest.

"Umph! Crap, I'm sorry." Large, strong hands wrap around my upper arms and hold me steady as I struggle to regain my footing. I reach down and adjust my shoe, then toss my hair back from my eyes and rise up to thank my rescuer. "Thank y…"

My words die in my throat as my eyes meet the same whiskey brown ones I've been lusting over for the past several days.

"Rafe?"

I don't know why I asked that. It's him.

It must be the booze talking.

The corner of his mouth quirks up in a sexy smirk. "Hello, Andy."

"Of all the gin joints…"

His eyes flare at my mumbled words, and he leans in closer, brushing his mouth against my ear. "…in all the towns in all the world, she has to walk into mine."

I sigh and practically sag against him.

How can knowing a movie quote be so fucking sexy?

"What are you doing here?" It's the only thing I can think to ask, because the words that really wanted to come out of my mouth were, "do you want to come home with me?"

He grins and steps closer, forcing me back against the wall. His arm presses next to my head and he leans in, hovering over me in all his masculine glory. The suit he wore earlier during our meeting has been replaced by a pair of dark, worn jeans and black button-down shirt that's open at the top, exposing the column of his neck and his lightly tanned skin at the base of his throat.

Christ, I want to lick that spot.

"I'm having dinner with my sister. What are *you* doing here?"

I giggle, *fucking giggle*, and lean my head back to look him in the eye. "I needed a drink after the week I had. Well, a drink or two...or is it three?"

A smile tilts the corners of his perfect lips. "That explains the stumble. You were so confident in those things earlier." He glances down at my Loubs, and I take the opportunity to examine his profile. The man is spectacularly handsome. Really. Like, he should be on the cover of a magazine not hosting a damn children's show. His strong, chiseled jaw and perfect straight nose, despite the blow to it, scream Roman elite.

I wonder if he has Italian blood?

When he returns his attention to me, the heat of his gaze reminds me why standing in a narrow, dark hallway with him is probably a bad idea. The sexual energy hums between us, and he lifts his hand to pull a strand of hair out of my face and tuck it behind my ear. The brush of his fingers against my skin sends a shiver of need through my body and straight to my core.

If there was any doubt about whether Rafe is feeling the same thing I am, it's gone the instant he steps forward and presses his growing erection against my lower belly.

Holy hell.

"Andy..." His warm breath flutters over me, his lips a mere inch from mine.

"Hmm?"

It takes every ounce of will-power I possess not to lean forward and kiss him. I want my lips on his more than I want to breathe right now.

"You're the boss. I'm an employee."

His words are like a bucket of ice cold water being dumped over my head. But he doesn't step back when he says it. He remains caging me in against the wall.

So I do the only thing I can. I state the obvious. "This is a really bad idea."

He nods, bringing his face even closer to mine, so close, I can feel the heat radiating off of him, and his soft pants of breath float across my cheek.

"A very bad one."

I suck in a deep breath, inhaling his natural scent mixed with some cologne that's making my lady parts tingle. "So what do we do?"

His mouth is on mine so fast, I barely have time to prepare myself for the attack. Lips press, tongues probe, bodies shift until we're practically dry-humping each other in the back of the restaurant.

Whatever is going on between us, it can't happen here.

I pull away and give myself a second to catch my breath. He eyes me warily, as if waiting for me to realize what he just did and fire him or something.

But that's the last thing I'm going to do. Instead, I'm going to risk both our careers. "1525 Bayshore Drive. Half an hour."

He grins and steps back, giving both of us space to move. His hand snakes down, and he adjusts his hard-on before holding out his arm for me to move in front of him back into the restaurant.

I step on wobbly legs but manage to remain upright. He stays several steps behind me, and out of the corner of my eye, I see him move to a table in the far corner where he joins a pretty brunette who's eyeing me from across the room.

My only hope is that we don't look as flustered as I feel. Because if we do, we are royally fucked.

9

"What the hell was that?" Riley narrows her dark eyes at me over the small table between us and gives me a *what the fuck* look.

I try to school my features as best I can when I meet her gaze. "What the hell was what?" I down half my glass of water to quench my suddenly parched mouth.

That woman sucks the breath right out of me. I don't remember the last time I made out with a woman in public and had to walk around in public like this with a damn erection like a teenage boy. It was probably high school or maybe college, certainly not in my adult life. Unless you count leaving Andy's office the last few days.

I don't know whether to be excited by it or terrified.

Riley tosses her thumb toward the hallway. "You go to the bathroom and then spend an inordinate amount of time in there. Then you come out immediately after a gorgeous blonde, who I'm pretty sure is your boss, with your pants looking too tight and her looking flushed."

I cough and adjust my raging erection.

Why the hell won't this thing go down?

I'm not in her orbit anymore, but my dick doesn't seem to have received the message yet. "I have no idea what you're talking about."

She sits back and crosses her arms over her chest. Riley has the best *you can't fuck with me* look. And she means it. Getting anything past her is tougher than getting a vegetarian to eat a steak.

"Knock it off, Rafe. Did you forget we shared a womb? You can't lie to me."

Fucking Riley.

She's like a dog with a bone. I know she won't let this go until she wrings the truth out of me. Just like she managed to convince me to come to dinner tonight when all I wanted to do was go home and drown myself in a bottle of bourbon. All it took were a few carefully worded threats involving Mom and telling her certain things we swore would stay between us for life before I was in a cab on my way here.

The woman is relentless, and as my twin sister, she also seems to think it's her job to meddle in my life on a constant basis. So there's no point in lying to her. She may even be able to offer some insight into the situation.

"That was, indeed, my boss."

Her eyebrows raise. "And…"

I sigh and run my hand through my hair as I recline back in my chair. "There's not much to tell. I met her a few days ago. There was a spark. She's my boss so I tried to ignore it. But the tension between us has grown palpable, and I just ran into her in the hallway by the bathrooms."

"Eww. You didn't fuck back there did you?"

Her scrunched up face almost makes me laugh but I can't find anything funny in this situation. Not after what's already happened the last few days.

"Do I look like some horn dog who can't keep my dick in my pants?"

The corner of her mouth ticks up. "No comment."

"Gee, thanks for the vote of confidence."

She shrugs and grins at me. It sucks how easily she can see right through me and how I have to let her get away with just about anything. "Well, if you didn't bone her, then what happened?"

Everything.

Nothing.

I don't know even know how to put it into words.

"I went to the bathroom. I came out. She came out. She stumbled on something, and I grabbed her to keep her from falling. There may have been some making out."

Riley's mouth drops open. "Making out? What are you, twelve?"

Fair question, and one I've already asked myself ten times.

Who does that? In public?

"Apparently, because we were kind of dry humping each other back there."

She bursts out laughing and slams her hand on the table, rattling the silverware and causing other patrons to glance over at us with disdain. "Jesus, this is a fucking trip and a half. My baby brother hung up and googley-eyed over a woman."

I give her my best stink eye at the "baby brother" remark. After thirty years, one would think she'd stop rubbing in that six minutes and thirty-two seconds.

"I'm not googley-eyed, just *intrigued*."

She sighs and waves her hand in my face. "Earth to Rafe. This is a really hella bad idea. The woman is your *boss* and you don't need to be thrust into the spotlight any more than you already are. Seriously, Rafe, stay away from that woman."

Riley's spot-on in her assessment of this situation, but the truth she just dumped on me does nothing to cool the raging fire of my lust for Andy. That woman is hell on heels, and I want to burn in the inferno that is her. Despite the risks, despite everything saying I shouldn't, I already know I'm going over there tonight. There's nothing in this world that could stop me.

10

I've paced and gone over this a hundred times while waiting for him, and despite all the reasons this is a terrible idea, I can't help thinking if we ignore this attraction, we will be missing out on something potentially amazing.

I need something amazing in my life. Yes, my job is incredible. But I need something for *me*. Someone to come home to, someone to love. And something about Rafe tells me this has potential.

There's no way I'm going to lose that. We'll deal with the fall out later.

The doorbell rings, and I have him inside and pressed against the door in two point five seconds flat.

What's the point in waiting?

We both know what we want. If he was having second thoughts, he would never have come tonight.

My mouth finds his while fervent hands work at his belt buckle.

He chuckles against my lips and weaves his hands into my hair to tug my head back. "Eager, are we?"

"Why wait?"

A grin that says *take me* spreads across his lips. "Good point." He tugs me back to him and presses his lips to mine in a searing kiss. His hands move to the zipper at the back of my dress and slide it down while I finish with his belt.

He reaches down to tug it off, but I pull it from his hand and wrap it around my wrist.

"We're going to need this."

His eyebrow raises, and it looks like he's about to ask me a question when I smash my mouth back to his. Tongues tangle. Hands grope, and we haven't even left the foyer yet.

My fingers move to his pants, and I work the zipper down, exposing his boxers and the raging hard-on encased in them. I brush my hand down the exposed part of his cock, and he shudders.

"We going to do this right here?" His words are breathless, and his racing heart under my palm assures me we are on the same page.

Thank God, because if he came here just to kiss me like this and leave, there wouldn't be enough batteries in the world to take care of my needs.

I chuckle against his lips. "I do have a giant bed."

He growls and grabs my hips, urging me to jump up and wrap myself around his waist. His hands dig into my ass as he steps away from the door. "Just give me directions, I'll get us there."

I have no doubt he can get me there. Just kissing him and having his hands on me has ramped me up so tight, it feels like I may explode at the first touch of his cock. I shift until the head of his cock brushes against my aching clit with every movement.

Rafe works his way toward the hallway. His lips leave a hot trail along my neck. "Where's the bedroom?"

"Third door on the right."

Although, I would have been fine with doing it right there against the door, or the wall, or on the floor, or the couch. It doesn't matter to me at this point. Nothing does but getting him naked and in me.

His hands grip my thighs as he walks us down toward the bedroom. Every movement sends the head of his cock brushing against my clit and shoots zings of pleasure through my core.

By the time he drops me on the bed, I'm practically panting and the lust burning in his dark eyes singes me everywhere he looks. Those eyes roam over me. "You have on way too many clothes."

I glance down at the dress bunched up around my waist and then at him in his pants and button down shirt. "I could say the same for you."

Quick fingers move down the buttons of his shirt, and he shrugs it back and off his arms, exposing his chiseled chest and abs. A light dusting of dark hair covers his pecs and trails down to the top of his boxers.

Watching his muscles bunch and flex while he undresses might as well be porn.

I shift on the bed, working my way out of my dress as he shoves down his pants and boxers.

His large, hard cock stands at attention between thick, muscular thighs.

Holy shit.

I clench my legs together against the throb there and beckon him to me with a curled finger.

The only thing separating us is the thin silk of my thong. He leans over me, and the heat radiating from his body warms me in the cool room.

Instead of lowering himself on top of me, he grabs my

ankles and tugs me to the edge of the bed. Even though I want him inside me, the look in his eyes promises I won't be disappointed with what he has to offer orally.

He licks his lips and drops to his knees. His fingers slip under my thong and he tugs it down my legs and tosses it over his shoulder.

A groan fills the room, and his hot breath fans across my overly-sensitive flesh. His tongue snakes out and the tip flicks my clit, sending a rush through my body.

"Holy hell."

This is going to be good.

11

Andy shudders under me, and I glide my tongue away from her clit and through her slick pussy.

Christ, she tastes so fucking good.

Like a fine wine, I want to savor every drop.

Her fingers twine into my hair, and she shifts, trying to guide me to where she wants me. But that's not happening. This is my opportunity to worship her, and I won't let her direct the show.

I reach up and slip a finger inside her slowly. She mewls and digs her fingers into my head. "Yes, God yes."

My tongue slides across her wet flesh, over and over, while I probe inside her. I add another finger and curl them into her G-spot. She pants and shifts under me, tugging at my head and begging me to shift my attentions.

She wants my mouth on her clit, but I'm enjoying bringing her up languidly. The slow build always leads to a better orgasm. And I want her to experience every fucking second of this, drawing it out as long as possible.

Licking.

Pulsing.

Probing.

Sucking.

Her hips buck when I finally flick my tongue over her engorged clit.

"Christ, Rafe, please!" The words are growled and combined with a sharp tug on my hair. The burn on my scalp urges me forward, finally giving her what she so desperately wants.

I suck her clit between my lips and start a relentless rhythm with my fingers in time with my mouth. She bows and flexes her hips into me, meeting my tempo and humping my face.

A few seconds later, she stills, her thighs tighten around my head, and she cries out. I continue the assault, dragging out her orgasm longer and harder.

She finally collapses and shoves my head away from her sensitive flesh.

Her lips curl up into a satisfied smile, and a laugh slips from her. "Fuck Rafe, that was incredible."

I rise to my feet and grip my aching cock in my hand.

Fuck if that didn't make me want to come all over the floor.

Having her fall apart like that with my touch makes my chest and dick swell to painful levels.

Her eyes follow my hand, and her tongue sneaks out and swipes across her lips. "Come here." She urges me onto the bed, and I comply, working my way up until I'm kneeling over her.

She leans forward and licks along my length. I release my cock, letting her swirl her tongue down around the root and all the way back to the head.

Fuck.

A shiver rolls down my spine, and my balls tighten up. "I won't last with you doing that, Andy."

Her glowing stare meets mine, and she grins. "I would love to suck your cum down, but I want this inside me more right now."

Christ. Who talks like that?

Andy apparently. And fuck if it isn't the sexist thing I've ever heard come from a woman's lips.

"That can be arranged." I pull back from her and move to drop down but she pauses me with a hand on my shoulder.

"Roll onto your back."

Andy gives me a gentle push, and I roll onto my back and shift up until my head hits the plush pillows. A sly grin spreads across her face as she comes up on her knees next to me. "Don't move."

I cross my hands behind my head and return her grin. "I wouldn't dream of it."

She slips off the bed and bends down to grab something. It dangles from her fingers ominously.

Holy shit. My belt.

I completely forgot she brought it into the bedroom with us and that she mentioned something about needing it later.

Her eyes flick up to the wrought-iron headboard behind me.

Oh hell no! She can't be serious.

With a chuckle, she climbs back up the bed and snaps the belt against her hand. "Put your hands together above your head."

Sweet Jesus, she is serious!

I can't say I've ever been tied up before during sex, or any other time for that matter. I trust Andy, but something about not being in control tugs at some very male part of me deep in my soul. The glint in her eye is what convinces me to let her, though. She's enjoying this, and all I want is to satisfy her.

I reach up and grab the headboard, wrapping my hands around the metal bars. She leans forward and weaves the belt around my wrists and the headboard, then tightens it until I can barely even shift them.

The satisfied smile on her face tells me all I need to know. I am in so much trouble, but it's the good trouble I'll be praying for again later.

She reaches into a side table and emerges with a condom, which she rolls down my length just slow enough to torture my engorged cock.

It throbs and pulses against my stomach, and I have to bite back the desire to beg her to touch me. I won't beg. Ever. Not even for this woman.

12

"Andy...please!"

It didn't take long for Rafe to beg. I'm actually a little disappointed at how easily he went from looking determined to begging for my pussy.

But I can't really blame him. I've been torturing him with gentle touches and brushing my wet core against him for at least ten minutes. The headboard and leather belt creak with every movement he makes and the sound makes my whole body clench.

I need him inside me as badly as he wants me, so I guess play time is done.

"Shh. I'll take care of you, Rafe." I lean forward and capture his mouth with mine. My tongue glides along his lips, requesting entrance. His lips slide open, allowing me in, and our tongues war, both demanding dominance. I finally pull away and grasp his cock, settling it at my wet core.

He gasps when I slip just the head inside me. I clench around him, and he groans. The headboard creaks. I slide down slowly, inch by glorious inch, letting his thick, hard cock stretch me.

"Fuck..." I drop my head back and savor the feeling of his big dick spreading me wide.

When he's finally seated all the way inside me, I pause for a moment and meet his eyes. Lust burns in their dark depths, a fire shimmering across the sea of bourbon. I squeeze around him, and his eyes roll back into his head.

"Christ, Andy, you feel so incredible."

I roll my hips and ease my way up his length. He groans and tugs at the restraints. "Let me out of this so I can touch you."

Tempting. But not yet.

I want to savor the control for another minute.

Another roll of my hips as I lower myself back down his cock has his hips bucking up to meet mine. I start a slow rhythm. Up and down. Rolling my hips and clenching my pussy around him.

His chest heaves, and his hips thrust up to meet mine with every pass.

I finally lean forward and unwrap the belt, freeing his wrists. His arms drop down, and he shakes his hands before they find my hips. Fingers dig into my flesh, and he drives up into me in earnest.

Every pump of his hips meets my downward thrust, sending him deep inside me. The head of his cock drags along my G-spot with each movement, sending ripples of pleasure coursing through my already sensitized body.

His pushes himself up on one hand and captures one of my nipples between his teeth. A soft nip sends me crashing over the edge again. My pussy clenches around him as wave after wave of pleasure takes me to oblivion.

He rolls us until I'm on my back and tugs my hips up,

giving himself the angle he needs to pound into me in a relentless tempo designed to find his own release.

Four hard pumps of his hips and he roars out my name, burying himself deep inside me. His head drops next to mine on the pillow, and his panting breaths fan against my ear.

No words are spoken. Because nothing needs to be said.

That was, without a doubt, the best sex I've ever had in my life. And it wasn't just because I haven't been laid in a while and needed to get off. No, it was because Rafe was so open, it allowed me to be completely free too. We just mesh. We fit together. And that's both thrilling and terrifying. The tightness in my chest only eases when he rolls off me to the side.

What if this was too much for him? The belt? The dominance.

He may run. It wouldn't be the first time.

He shifts up from the bed and disappears into the adjoining bathroom. When he returns, I'm almost afraid to look at him, but the grin on his face sends a jolt of relief through me.

No man grins like that unless he's satisfied and enjoyed himself. No man.

Rafe crawls back into bed and over to me until he's resting his head against my shoulder.

"Well, that was certainly...a new experience."

My laugh joins his and the sound fills the room.

"Is that a compliment or an insult?"

He pushes up on his elbows and presses a kiss to my temple. "Very much a compliment."

"Mmm. Good." I burrow deeper into the pillows and roll onto my side to face him. "Because insulting your boss would probably be bad for your career."

He bursts out laughing and rolls onto his back, dropping an arm over his eyes. "Shit, don't remind me of how complicated this situation is, please. Just let me enjoy the aftereffects of this. I need it after this week."

"Did you ever watch the video from the game?"

His head jerks up, and he looks over at me. "What? Hell no! I don't want to see that shit."

I crawl over to him and grin. "I can understand that. Let me just tell you, the camera doesn't do you justice." My eyes drift down to his semi-hard dick, which twitches at my words.

"Oh really?"

I lick my lips and smile as I work my way down his body. "Really. And I'd love a repeat performance."

13

Waking up next to a beautiful woman is never a bad thing. The morning sunlight streaming in through the open curtains finally spurs me into action, and I roll over toward her.

Her blonde hair fans out like a halo around her face, and the soft rise and fall of her chest tells me she's still sleeping.

She has to be exhausted after last night and this morning. I sure am. I didn't know I had it in me for four rounds. It's more than I've gone in a long time.

Andy is insatiable, and she gets what she wants. I have no complaints and neither does my dick because, frankly, that was the best sex I've ever had.

Her complete lack of inhibitions made everything ten times more intense. Most women are so afraid of doing or saying something embarrassing during sex that they never fully let go, but not Andy.

From the moment I walked in the door and she slammed me back against it, she took what she wanted, what she needed.

Fuck, that was so hot.

There's just something about a woman who takes command. And Andy is precisely the type who will take the reins and send you galloping. Boy did she ride me hard. My cock feels like it's gone ten rounds in the ring with Ali.

I slink out of bed and into the bathroom, grabbing my phone along the way. I don't want to wake her up, and my messages can probably wait, but after days of being disconnected from the world intentionally, I'm starting to get antsy. The response to the press conference seemed good from what I saw last night before I got here. And I'm hoping the good press continues.

The door clicks shut behind me, and I flip on the light. The man staring back at me in the mirror looks as exhausted as I feel. Thank God it's Saturday, and I don't have anything on my schedule today.

If Andy's game, I plan on staying in bed with her all day and working on what we started last night.

But any plans for the day fly out the window the second I open my phone and see seventy-four missed calls and sixty-three text messages from Riley, Mom, and a ton of my friends and co-workers.

Shit.

This can't be good. There are even more than immediately after the wardrobe malfunction. That dragged people out of the woodwork, so whatever this is must be pretty fucking epic.

I scroll through my voicemails until I find the most recent one from Riley, and I play it.

"Rafe. Where the hell are you? I've been texting and calling you for hours. You need to check out The A List immediately. They have pictures. It's bad."

The message ends abruptly.

Pictures? Pictures of what?

They already have ones of my dick, what could possibly be worse? A million possibilities flip through my mind as I pull up my web browser but nothing prepares me for what I see when I open the main page to the celebrity gossip site, The A List.

Me and Andy in the hallway at the restaurant humping each other.

Her hand on my crotch.

My hand on her ass.

Kissing.

Groping.

We look like the horny teenagers we were acting like. And it isn't flattering for either of us. It makes me look like a sex-crazed pervert and her look like a slut.

Where the fuck did they get these?

Why would they even bother?

The quality is low and somewhat grainy in the dark hallway, but you can clearly tell it's us. It had to be from a surveillance camera in the hall, but how would anybody have access to this? Why would anybody care?

Jesus Christ.

The headline is just as bad if not worse than the pictures.

Rafe Boswell doesn't just show his dick to kids and families at charity events, he apparently uses it to keep his job too...

Fucking A, who writes this stuff?

How did I let this happen?

I knew this was a bad idea for both of us, but I was thinking with my dick and not my head.

I need to get out of here and start doing some damage control.

The first stop on the list is that restaurant to find out who got this videotape. I'll figure out the rest later.

I toss my phone on the counter and drop my head down. This has, without a doubt, been the worst week of my life. How can the best twelve hours be crammed in between so much bullshit? And something tells me it's only going to get worse before it gets better.

Splashing cold water on my face doesn't cool my boiling blood. I need to get the hell out of here.

I make my way to the bedroom and see Andy's still sleeping peacefully. Logic says I should wake her to tell her what's going on, but frankly, I'm so pissed off, I would probably say something I regret. Which is bad when she's my boss and I just slept with her...repeatedly.

Dammit.

This is exactly the type of entanglement I wanted to avoid. But she drew me to her like a moth to a flame. I was sucked in by the heat and vibrancy and now, I'm getting burned.

With one last look back at her, I slip on my jeans and shirt and make my way out without saying goodbye.

14

I roll onto my stomach and reach out for Rafe but that side of the bed has nothing but cold sheets.

He's been gone for a while. And there's no water running in the bathroom. Which means he left.

What the hell?

I push up into my elbows and search the room for any sign of a note or something. Nada.

He fucking ghosted me!

Jerk.

Why would he just take off?

Last night was amazing, for me anyway. I can't remember the last time I came so much or so hard. I would have thought he would want to stay for a repeat performance. But maybe I just read too much into it. Maybe he needed to scratch the itch. Or maybe my dominance scared the shit out of him and he was just waiting for the right moment to sneak away.

That's more likely considering my history with men. I had just hoped Rafe was different. He certainly didn't seem to mind what I was doing last night, taking control and directing him. He seemed to enjoy it actually.

So what the hell happened?

He left you high and dry and smelling like sweaty, raunchy sex.

And now you'll have to go in on Monday and pretend nothing happened.

Fucking awkward. Way to go, Andy.

At least he has no reason to be in my office now that CockGate is done and over with. It's not like he will be wandering around the corporate offices. He spends most of his time down on his set and I spend mine in the boardroom.

Don't let this affect your professional relationship with him.

It doesn't matter that he hurt me. There were no promises made. I really can't hold anything against him at this point. We had fun, and that's all I can ask for, I guess.

That doesn't really calm the ache in my chest, but I force myself out of bed and into the bathroom for a shower.

The scalding hot water soothes my sore muscles. Last night was a real fucking workout. By far the most cardio I've done in a long time. And I am feeling it everywhere, especially between my legs. But it's a good ache. That deep one that reminds you of how amazing it was.

Too bad I won't get a repeat.

A quick soaping and some shampoo and conditioner later, I climb from the shower and towel off before heading back to the bedroom to check my messages. I turned my ringer off last night, something I almost never do in case of an emergency, but I wanted my night with Rafe to be uninterrupted.

The sheer number of missed calls and messages tells me that may have been a mistake.

What the hell is going on?

The last three texts are from Penny.

9:15 am

CALL ME!

9:21 am

CALL ME!

9:23 am

CALL ME!

I dial her and sit back on the bed, bracing myself for whatever bad news I know she has for me.

"Andy! Jesus! Where the hell have you been? The shit is hitting the fan and you went dark! What the hell am I saying, I know exactly where you've been—"

"Penny, what's going on? Why all the calls?"

She lets out a long sigh, and I can practically see her burying her face in her hand. "The A List posted pictures early this morning. Pictures of you and Rafe in a very compromising position. It looks like a hallway somewhere."

Oh hell...

Visions of our dry-humping at the restaurant fill my head.

"Shit."

"Yeah, Andy, it's not good. All the celeb sites are running articles saying he hooked up with you to try to save his job and that's the only reason you stood up for him and kept him on at the network."

"Double shit." I drop my head in my hand and scrub it down my face.

Fuck, fuck, fuck, fuck!

I drop back onto the bed that still smells like sex and wish I could just fall back into that blissful, post-sex sleep and forget about the impending A-bomb about to go off at the network.

"Has anyone from the board seen it yet?"

"Yes. Barry called two hours ago and requested an emergency board meeting this afternoon at two."

I glance at the clock. I have three hours to get myself together and try to figure out a plan.

"Okay, thanks for the heads up. No statements to anyone. Got it?"

"I got it, Andy. I'll see you soon."

Shit. Shit. Shit.

My phone hitting the wall across the room makes a resounding thud but it doesn't give me the satisfaction of shattering like I had intended. The desire to smash something overwhelms me, and the lamp on my nightstand ends up absorbing my rage. It shatters against the wood floor in a satisfying crack and pieces fly everywhere.

This is bad. This is career-ending kind of bad. And I walked right into it by taking Rafe into my bed.

Now I have to spend the next couple hours on the phone with the legal department trying to put out this fire, but I fear the flames have already engulfed me.

15

"What do you mean you don't know?"

The manager of the restaurant shrugs and holds his hands up. "I'm sorry, man. I have no idea how someone got the video. All the employees have access to the back office during their shifts, so really, anyone could have gone in there and taken it."

You've got to be fucking kidding me?

What kind of business leaves the office wide open for just anyone to waltz in there and take something like a security video?

"Can't you check the cameras to see who went back there?"

He shakes his head. "We use digital recording and everything from last night was deleted after they took the video you're talking about. Someone knew what they were after apparently."

Jesus. This can't be happening.

Some asshole waiter probably recognized us and decided to make a few extra bucks by selling the video to those sleazeballs over at The A List.

And now my career is definitely over. There's no coming back from something like this. Yes, people in Hollywood make mistakes, a lot of them, but not kids' show hosts. It's one thing if you're a big movie star or even on a sitcom, but I sit and talk to kids. They can't have someone who comes across as a sex-crazed pervert hosting a show on their network. Period.

"Thanks for nothing, asshole." I push away from the bar and shove my hands back through my hair. It's not his fault. I know that logically, but I can't think with logic right now. My life is crumbling. All because of a damn basketball game.

If I had hooked up with Andy under any other circumstances, there wouldn't be a story there. It would just be two consenting adults who decided to sleep together. But the dickslip has turned this into something enormous.

I push my way out of the restaurant and dig my phone out of my pocket. I've ignored the calls and messages all morning while I cleaned up and made my way over here, but now, it's time to face the music.

The last few hours have made me realize there's no damage control here. I'm toast. I can call The A List to make a statement that any relationship between Andy and me is totally irrelevant to what happened with the network, but the words will be empty. This is the type of situation that doesn't have a positive outcome.

At least karma could have used some lube.

I dial the only person I can think of to call, because God knows, I can't deal with Riley right now, and she would usually be my first call.

"Rafe? Dude! Where the hell have you been? I've been calling all morning." Hearing Nate's voice does nothing to soothe my frayed nerves like I thought it would.

Shouldn't talking to your best friend make you feel better?

Maybe it's because I know he won't beat around the bush with me, and that means I'm walking into a very uncomfortable conversation.

My car door slams shut behind me, and I crank it to life. "I've been trying to figure out who leaked the pictures."

"Any luck?"

"No." I merge into traffic and make my way back toward my condo. "It was probably just some waiter or someone who recognized us and wanted some quick money. It's my fault for getting involved with Andy in the first place, let alone manhandling her in public. What the fuck was I thinking?"

Nate snorts. "You weren't thinking, dude. At least not with the head above your waist. Seriously, she's your *boss*."

I slam my hand against the steering wheel and stop at a red light. "I know. I knew it was a bad idea from the moment I set foot in her office."

He sighs. "But you did it anyway."

"I did it anyway."

How could I not?

The attraction between us was unlike anything I've ever felt, a physical pull, dragging me along against my own free will. "Can you blame me, though?"

Another snort laugh echoes through the phone, and I can see Nate with his feet propped up on his desk, his phone tucked between his ear and shoulder. "She's hot. I'll give you that. But seriously, man. Really bad fucking timing."

"No shit, Sherlock."

"So what are you going to do?"

Isn't that the big question? What *do* I do next?

"I guess I turn in my resignation before they fire me, and

then I crawl into a hole until this all blows over and then try to figure out what to do with the rest of my life."

"You could always go back to the museum, can't you?"

Visions of the bowels of the Natural History Museum flood my mind. It's not that I didn't love working there, because I really did. But after having so much fun the last two years, combining my love for science and history with being in front of the camera, I don't know how to go back to cataloguing bones. I guess I could get back into doing digs, but that was never my forte. At least it would be more interesting than standing in the lab all day.

"Yeah, I'm sure they would take me back. But I'm not sure that's the right place for me anymore."

"Well, you need to do something, buddy. What are you going to do about the chick? How did you leave things?"

The chick...

Memories from last night flash before my eyes. Her hovering over me. Her riding me. Me pounding into her from behind. Her doing that thing with her legs I didn't think was physically possible...

My cock rises in my pants as I pull into my parking space.

I just left her there. Without a fucking word.

Christ, I'm a dick.

"I could have left things better."

Understatement of the year.

16

I don't think I've ever seen so many angry faces all focused at me.

The board is pissed.

And I can't say I blame them.

Not only is this a huge scandal for the network because of Rafe, but I slept with an employee, one I spent hours singing the praises of only a few days ago. Of course, this looks bad. Very, very bad.

Frankly, it's probably unsalvageable. But damn if I'm not going down without a fight.

"I know how bad this looks—"

"Bad?" Barry stands and slams his palm down on the conference table. "Bad doesn't even *begin* to describe this situation, Andrea. What were you thinking?"

I take a deep, calming breath before responding.

Don't snap back at him.

"First and foremost, I need to make sure it's clear that nothing happened between me and Mr. Boswell prior to last evening. I stood up for him and his position here because I genuinely believe in his brand and that it is an asset to the network. That being said, yes, we let things get too far last night. I shouldn't have become romantically involved with an employee."

"You're damn right you shouldn't have! Not only is it against company policy, but it opens us up to lawsuits from Mr. Boswell as well as even more scrutiny in the press. This is a catastrophe!"

Exaggerate much?

Sure, it's bad. I can't deny that. But catastrophe is a pretty strong word. An earthquake is a catastrophe. A hurricane is a catastrophe. This was a bad decision and bad timing.

"That's a bit of an overstatement, Barry. This can be salvaged."

His bushy eyebrows raise. "Salvaged? And how the hell do you think that's going to happen?"

I rise from my chair and move to stand behind it. I'm not giving him the satisfaction of towering over me and looking down on me. "I will give a statement admitting to a consensual romantic encounter with Rafe Boswell and make it clear this had nothing to do with the network standing behind him after the incident at the game."

Barry huffs out a snort-laugh. "God, you are naïve, Andrea. A statement at this point is worthless. Even if we could get Rafe on board by having him sign an affidavit that your 'encounter' was consensual, the damage to our reputation and to both of yours has been done."

I can see where this is going. I knew it was coming the moment I saw the pictures with my own eyes. But something in me hoped the board would listen to reason and give me a chance to try to fix things.

"I know what you're going to say, Barry. And don't bother. I will resign before I ever let the board fire me. I'm sure you all discussed this before I ever got here today. I could tell the moment I set foot in this room you had already made your decision. Just know it's a mistake. I'm exactly what this network needs, and a little sex scandal would never get in the way of my plans. I'm disappointed you have such narrow minds that you can't see that."

The only response I get is silence, which means I hit the nail right on the head. They wrote me off the minute those pictures surfaced. I was already on rocky ground with the whole Rafe fiasco, and this just cemented my fate.

There's a good chance I'll never work in television again after this.

Fucking A. I sure made a mess out of this.

I wish I could blame it on the booze, but I knew full well what I was doing and the risk I was taking letting Rafe into my bedroom. This is precisely what we *both* knew could happen. I just never imagined someone would actually care enough to rat us out.

Only one name pops into my head. Munro. The man is devious, and while I'm sure he wasn't personally at the restaurant grabbing the recording, chances are good he had feelers out and had spread the word to be on the look-out for anything that could be used to take Rafe down. And we handed it to him on a silver fucking platter.

The board members shift uncomfortably in their seats while they wait for me to say something or to leave.

Good. Let them be uncomfortable.

I hold my ground and wait for Barry to speak. He eyes me for a few moments before he finally heaves in a breath and steps back from the table. "I'm sorry it has to end like this, Andrea. We had high hopes for you with the network and what the fresh perspective could offer. But remember, it's you who put you in this situation, not us."

Yeah right, if a male CEO slept with a female host, they

would probably be smacking him on the back and congratulating him even though it was a violation of company policy.

I almost say as much but bite my tongue instead. There's no need to go out on a bad note, or one any worse than what it is already at least.

At this point, I still have some dignity, and I'll be damned if I let the board take that from me.

I step back from my chair and nod. "You'll have my formal resignation this evening."

Those are certainly words I never expected to say. I've never had to resign to save my ass from being fired. Regret burns in my gut as I turn on my heels and march from the conference room with my head held high.

I don't want to regret what happened with Rafe. It was too good to now be tied to such a shit outcome. But there's no going back to that shameless flirtation or mindless sex. Not after this. Even if I still wanted him, there's no way this won't blacken every moment we ever spend together in the future.

Those pictures weren't just the end of my career. They were the end to anything I ever hoped to have with Rafe.

17

"Move."

Riley raises her eyebrow and fails to budge from her seat on the couch...in my favorite spot.

"Don't make me move you. You may be older, but I'm bigger and stronger."

She sighs and sticks her tongue out at me before sliding over to the other end of the couch with her plate in hand.

I drop into my usual spot and flip on the television. "I assume you want to watch the game?"

"Duh." The word somehow manages to make it out around the piece of pizza shoved in her mouth.

I find the Kings game and relax back into the plush leather with my own slice. It's been a hell of a couple days, and all I want to do is enjoy the game in peace. Of course, I hadn't expected my nosy sister to appear at my door half an hour ago.

At least she brought wine. I can forgive the intrusion since she brought booze. Plus, I made her promise not to discuss my recent exploits and unemployment.

I should have known that was an empty promise. My sister is nothing if not tenacious.

"You really just left her in bed and never even called or anything?"

"Jesus Christ, Riley!" I toss my pizza back on the plate and glare at her. "You couldn't leave it alone, could you?"

She holds her hands out. "What? What did I do?"

"You promised you wouldn't bring it up."

Her plate lands on the coffee table, and she turns toward me. "I'm sorry, Rafe, but I feel like this is something that you need to talk about and face. You had an amazing night with this woman and then just left her in the dust as soon as shit got real. That's a real dick move."

Like I don't know that.

I've spent the last two days regretting every move I made that morning, but it's not like I can take it back. "What's done is done, Riley. Let it be."

She grins at me and shakes her head. "No can do, little bro. I'm a woman. We don't let things go, which is why I know that Andy is probably reeling from what happened. She lost her *job* over this, over standing up for you and acting on whatever the attraction between you was. That's a big deal. And to wake up to all that turmoil and not even have you there, not even a note, that's pretty fucked up."

"If I wanted a sermon, I would have gone to church with Mom."

"Ouch. I'm not trying to lecture you, here. I just think you need to at least call this woman and give her an explanation and an apology. You weren't the only one whose life was affected by all this."

No shit.

I may have been forced to resign, but I wasn't the CEO of

a multi-million dollar network like Andy. She didn't stand a chance once those pictures got out.

And it's not that I don't feel like a dick for how I left things, it's more that I feel so awful about it, I don't even know how to go about contacting her.

What the hell would I even say? I had the best night of my life, I'm sorry it cost both of us everything?

"What would I say to her, Riley?"

She leans forward, grabs her pizza, and takes an enormous bite before answering me. "You tell her the truth. Explain why you left so suddenly and why you didn't call or come back."

"You mean tell her I totally panicked and didn't know what to do? Yeah, that's a fabulous idea."

There's a brief moment of silence while she chews another bite. Then she dives right back in, eliminating my momentary reprieve. "If that's the truth, then yeah. There's no shame in admitting you panicked. I probably would have too in that situation, but really, Rafe, you should have woken her up and you two should have dealt with this *together*."

I scrub my hands over my face and then move my plate to the table. My appetite has vanished quicker than I did from her bedroom. "I know that. That's why I feel like such a fucking ass."

"How did you leave things with the network? All you told me was you quit before they could fire you."

"I dropped off a letter of resignation. Two hours later, I got a call from someone in the legal department asking me to sign something that said Andy never sexually harassed me or coerced me into sleeping with her."

Riley's jaw drops and she gasps. "Did you sign it?"

I scoff and glare at her. "Of course I did. Andy didn't do anything wrong, at least, other than violating corporate policy. I get that sleeping with someone you are superior to creates all sorts of implications, so I know why they needed a release. I would never want her to get into trouble for what I did, and I'm not some asshole who would use what happened between us for my own gain by suing the damn network."

She chuckles and takes another bite of her pizza. "Why the hell not. You could be set for life."

The pillow I throw hits her square in the face, and she practically chokes on her food.

"Not funny, Riley."

She shrugs and grins at me. "I thought it was funny."

It was a little funny, but I can't bring myself to laugh about that right now. I can't laugh about anything. My life has fallen apart so quickly, I'm barely standing. And the way things are between me and Andy only makes it worse.

18

"Girl, you have *got* to get up off that couch."

I glare at Jenna and shake my head, burrowing deeper into the pillows and blankets. "No."

"At least take a shower. You smell like that homeless guy who always begs on the corner by Starbucks."

As surreptitiously as possible, I sniff my shirt. Maybe I do need a shower, or at least a change of clothes. But it's not like I'm going anywhere. I haven't even left the house in three days. There's no point.

Any career I had is gone. I just need a few days to wallow in self-pity before I decide what to do with my life.

"Seriously, get up. We're going out."

I glance down at myself then back at Jenna. My leggings and old t-shirt aren't exactly going out attire. I also haven't showered in enough days that I can't remember the actual count. "Out? No. I will agree to shower, but we can order something to eat. I'm not leaving the house."

She sighs and drops down on the couch by my feet. "Fine. But tell me, are you ever going to get your ass out of this house and back to life?"

"What's the point? I don't have a job, my reputation is non-existent, and the only man I've been involved with for months left me high and dry with a major crisis."

"He still hasn't called, huh?"

I shake my head and stare at the silent phone sitting on my coffee table. Nothing. Nada. Zip. Zero. Zilch. Not a call or a text to touch base or to see how I'm doing. The man just disappeared.

Part of me argues that I can't really blame him. He woke up in my bed to his world imploding and it was partially my fault. The other part of me wants to rip his balls off and shove them down his throat for walking away instead of facing the fallout of our actions together.

That part of me has been winning out over the last couple days.

"Why don't you call him?"

I whip my head around to her and see she's totally serious. "What? You're crazy. I'm not calling the guy who snuck out after a night of amazing sex when both our worlds were falling apart around us without so much as a warning or good morning."

She shrugs. "Why the hell not? It's clear you need some sort of closure on this whole thing. Just handing in your resignation and walking away from the job may have ended that, but it didn't end whatever you had with Rafe."

What did I have with Rafe?

Attraction...yes.

Lust...definitely.

But was there more there?

I certainly would like to think so, but what can I really know after one night. He never gave us the chance to see where this might go before he bolted. I want to believe it was just because of the pictures leaking, and had that not happened, I would have woken to a warm body next to me. Rafe doesn't seem the type to sneak away, so I'll give him the benefit of the doubt on that.

But that doesn't lessen the sting nor does it explain why he hasn't gotten in contact since then.

Maybe he's scared I blame him for what happened. It would be logical he might think I would feel that way. But he hasn't even given me a chance to explain that I don't blame him. I know my own actions and choices are what got me here.

There's no denying that. We both played a role, but I could have stopped things at the restaurant. I could have done what a good boss is supposed to do and reject his advances. But I so badly wanted to know what it would feel like to be in his arms, to have him inside me. I let caution fly out the window along with my career.

And now, I'm paying the price. Literally and figuratively.

Lucrative and prestigious job...gone.

Potential at finding a real relationship with someone I click with...gone.

I can't just call him.

Can I?

"You really think I should just call him?"

Jenna sighs and pours herself a glass of wine from the bottle on the coffee table. "I think you won't get off this couch to do more than eat, shit, and piss until you do."

"Geez, crude much?"

Her eyebrow raises, and she takes a sip of her wine. "Am I wrong?"

"That's beside the point."

She grins over the glass at me. "Just say it. I promise not to lord it over you for too long. Just admit I'm right."

I cross my arms over my chest and return my attention

to whatever mindless crap is on the T.V. "Over my dead body."

"From the smell of it, you're getting close anyway."

I throw a wadded up tissue at her. "Bitch."

She shrugs and smiles. "I may be a bitch, but I'm a bitch who is one hundred percent right about this. Call the man."

19

Three weeks later

I never thought I'd be back here, in the bowels of the museum digging through boxes of uncategorized bones.

Life can change so damn fast...

But at least I was able to land on my feet. The museum jumped at the chance to get me back, even with the swirl of scandal still lingering around me. Things have died down for the most part, though. I guess that's the one good thing about L.A., a scandal never lasts for long here. It's immediately replaced by something more tantalizing that will sell more magazines and papers and get more clicks.

The only lingering issue is how I left things with Andy.

I can't forget the way she looked spread out across the bed that morning, her honeysuckle scent invading my nose, her nails scoring down my back, or the way her pussy felt wrapped around my cock.

My cock swells just thinking about it, the same way it

has a hundred times over the last several weeks. Dr. Boner has become quite an apt name, all because of that sexy, feisty blonde.

I've thought about calling her a hundred times, but ultimately, my own pride has kept me from contacting her. That and wondering if she blames me for what happened. I should have walked away when she fell on me in that hallway. I should have righted her on her heels and sent her on her merry way. But no, I had to have her. And it cost me everything, including my sanity. Because I can't get her out of my head.

Trying to shake off the memories of that night is useless. I just need to learn to live with them and without her.

At least I have these bones to work on. I would be lying if I said I wasn't giddy at the thought of assembling another skeleton from some prehistoric beast. It's been years since I've been able to do this, and my hands practically itch digging through the hundreds of years of boxes in the basement to see what we have. So many things have been donated and mislabeled over the years, the museum doesn't even know what it has. I jumped at the chance to come back and dig through all this stuff.

It's the next most exciting thing to hosting my show, and it's my first true love. What little boy doesn't dream of digging up dinosaur bones and holding something millions of years old? Most people never get to see or touch the things I have in my hands right now, and looking down at the femur, the regrets I feel for what's happened the last month seem to lighten.

I'm going to be okay.

The ringing of my phone forces me to set the bone down and dig in my pocket.

If it's Riley again, I swear to God...

An unknown number flashes across my screen. I'm tempted to hit ignore and get back to work. I've had enough calls from reporters and friends over the past four weeks to last me a lifetime. But a nagging feeling in the pit of my stomach tells me to answer it.

"Hello?"

Silence greets me, and I almost hang up. Telemarketing scum.

"Rafe?"

Her voice draws me back to the phone and almost stops my heart.

"Andy?"

Another silence lingers over the line. *Is she going to say something? Why is she calling?*

"Andy? Are you okay?"

She sighs and gives a mirthless laugh. "Define okay."

The table behind me lets out a creak of protest as I lean back against it. "That doesn't sound good."

"Look, I called because I thought I could just get over what happened but it's been a month and I still think about it every damn day."

She's not the only one. And that's the last thing I expected her to say. This is my chance, my opportunity to apologize for being such a huge dick. "I'm sorry."

A laugh trickles through the phone and goes straight to my cock. That damn laugh. I've dreamt about that laugh for weeks and wondered if I would ever hear it again. Now, I'd give anything to have her here so I can see her when we have this conversation and experience it in person.

"For what? Leaving me alone in bed without a word? Hooking up with me in the first place?"

Ouch. I guess I deserve that.

"For being a huge dick and bailing on you when I saw those pictures."

"Yeah, you were kind of a dick."

I kick my feet out in front of me and cross my ankles. "I know. And I really am sorry. I've wanted to call a hundred times, but I just figured you'd be so pissed you wouldn't want to hear from me."

She sighs again, and the frustration is evident even though we're miles apart. "I was more hurt than pissed. We could have dealt with things together, you know."

"Yeah, I do know. I realized that after I had already left and gone to the restaurant to try to figure out who leaked the tape. But by then, I knew I was losing my job and you probably were too, and I just wanted to wallow in self-pity. Plus, I knew it was a dick move to leave and I was too embarrassed to face you."

"Can you face me now?"

20

It takes him a second to react to my voice behind him. He lowers the phone from his ear and turns slowly until he's facing me.

"Hi."

God, that was hella lame, Andy.

I've practiced what I would say to him a thousand times but as soon as he's standing in front of me, I can't manage anything more than *hi*.

His dark eyebrows raise, and he slips his phone onto the table in front of him. I definitely surprised him. And that's exactly what I wanted. I wanted to catch him off guard so I could gauge his real reaction to me. "What are you doing here? How did you find me?"

Shit. What am I doing?

I already got my apology. Maybe I should have let it go at that. "Um, I wanted to talk to you. And I called the museum hoping you had come back to work here. They told me you were back. Someone led me down here when I arrived."

He examines me, his eyes roving over me from head to foot. I wasn't sure what the proper attire was for confronting the guy who abandoned you after an amazing night of hot sex, so I went with a cute skirt and a wrap top that shows off my tits. At the very least, I can show him what he left.

But he hasn't said anything, and the tension in the air is starting to frazzle my nerves more than I'd like to admit.

"Do you want me to go?"

My question snaps him back, and he shakes his head. "No, I'm just…really surprised to see you. I thought you wouldn't ever want to see me again after the way we left things."

"The way *you* left things."

He sighs and pushes his hand back through his hair. "Yes. The way *I* left things."

At least he's admitting he was a dick here. I thought I'd be more angry when I saw him for the first time, but the only thing I feel right now is the pull of ardent attraction between us. Even now, after everything that's happened, it's still there, beckoning me to him.

One step, then another, and another drive me closer to him, around the edge of the table until I'm standing in front of him.

He's just as devastatingly handsome as he was that first day in my office, and now that I know what he has happening under all those clothes, it's hard not to imagine what he looked like naked and tied up in my bed.

"How mad are you?"

I shake my head and press my palms against his chest. "I'm not mad. I was hurt, then I got mad, then I kind of got over it. We both lost a lot because of our choices."

That's an understatement, but the truth, nonetheless.

Rafe sighs and reaches up to tuck a strand of hair behind my ear. The familiar movement sends flashes of that night through my head, and my body heats at the memories.

His hand lingers against my cheek, and he watches me like he's waiting for some response.

"What do we do now?" His words are nothing more than a whisper, but the question is one I've been asking myself over and over again.

I reach up and press my hand over his. "Well, we either say our goodbyes or..."

The words catch in my throat. I'm not usually one to hold back, but with everything that's happened with Rafe, it feels like unsteady ground.

His thumb brushes over my cheek. "Or?"

Suck it up and say it, Andy.

"Or, you kiss me and we see where this goes."

He doesn't react right away, just stares at me with something akin to wonder in his dark eyes. "You're willing to forgive and forget so easily?"

I shake my head and grin at him. "Oh, I forgive you, but I won't forget. You'll pay me back in other ways."

A million different ideas take hold. Some involving his belt again.

Damn, that was hot. We were hot. Scalding.

And I pray I'm not throwing myself out on a limb here for something that will never happen again. I can understand if he doesn't want to get involved with me. It would be a constant reminder of the clusterfuck we created. One I'm still trying to recover from.

The fact that I'm still jobless weighs heavily on me but not as much as how things were left with Rafe. But now, standing here staring at him, I'm wondering if maybe this was a mistake.

I pull my hand back down and shift away from him, but instead of letting me go, he steps into me, pressing his chest against mine and stopping his lips mere millimeters from mine.

His warm breath fans over my mouth. He smells like peppermint, and the scent swirling around me only reminds me more of our night together.

A shudder rolls through my body, and I clench my legs together to help dull the aching throb there.

Something very hard and warm presses into my stomach, and he takes my face between his palms, tilting my head up until I meet his eyes again.

"Don't go."

It's all I wanted to hear. Well, that and the apology I already received.

Before I can respond, his lips descend on mine. The sweet kiss doesn't remain soft and light. It deepens quickly, his lips and tongue demanding against my own.

A groan rumbles in his chest, and he walks me backward until my ass hits the edge of the table. Something on the table rolls and the legs wobble slightly.

He chuckles against my mouth. "I hope this table holds up. I have plans for you."

21

My body molds into her warm one as I press her back against the table.

I never thought I'd see her again, let alone have her under me and practically begging me to take her.

This woman is so incredible. Her ability to move on from what happened without looking back blows my fucking mind. She forgave me. Just like that.

But the gleam in her eye tells me she won't ever let me forget what I did. I'll be paying for it for as long as we're together. Funny thing is, I don't mind that. I deserve it, really.

And right now, she's in my domain and she's looking up at me with a smirk that screams *take me now*. Her legs wrap up around my waist, and she rubs her hot core against my cock. Even through the fabric of my pants, it sears my hard flesh and makes it throb.

Weeks of dreaming about her, about us, about this, have left my willpower non-existent. She deserves to be in a soft bed with pillows and crisp sheets, not spread out across a dusty, dirty table and surrounded by boxes full of dinosaur bones. But I can't wait. I won't wait. Not after this long.

Her eyebrow quirks up. "Are you going to just stand there staring at me, or are you going to fuck me?"

Holy shit.

She doesn't need to ask me twice.

Her legs fall, and I reach between us and unbuckle my belt, then shove down my pants and boxers in one swift motion. My cock springs free, and she groans and shifts to wrap her legs around me again. They squeeze around me. I brush my hands up her thighs, shifting her skirt even higher, and my breath catches in my throat.

Jesus. She's not wearing panties.

Moisture glistens on her pussy. She's already wet for me, and fuck if that doesn't make my cock jump.

"Christ, Andy." I brush my finger through her slick folds and she bucks under me. She needs this just as badly as I do, and I'm more than willing to give it to her, even here.

Her small hand reaches up and wraps around my cock. She licks her lips.

Fuck, I want that mouth wrapped around my dick, but not right now. Right now, I want to be buried inside her so deep, she'll feel me for weeks.

A single brush of her thumb across the head has a feral growl rumbling from my lips. "You're mine, Andy. I don't care about what happened or what anyone else thinks about us being together. This, us, is good…great. And I'm not going to make the mistake of walking away again."

She grins and swirls her thumb again. "Then shut up and kiss me."

In a split second, my lips are on hers. I kiss her with a passion I didn't know I possessed, probing, licking, sucking, demanding. And she gives it all back in return.

Her grip on my dick tightens, and she strokes along the length over and over, bringing me practically to the breaking point. But I'm not coming on her hand or over her stomach. I'm going to be buried inside her when I come.

I jerk out of her grip and position myself at her warm, wet entrance. Her eyes lock on mine and the spark there, the deep lust and need for me shining in their depths, sends me driving into her.

Her head drops back, and a gasp slips from her mouth. "God, Rafe!"

The tight, wet heat of her pussy clasps at me and ripples along my cock. She squeezes as I pull out, creating a vise-like grip on my flesh and driving me to plunge into her even harder the second time.

She bucks and shifts under me, drawing me closer with her heels digging into my lower back. Thrust after relentless thrust, I drive into her, pushing her down onto the old, wooden table. It creaks and groans under the stress, and the boxes on it rattle and shift.

Every pump of my hips drives my cock deeper and harder. Her pussy clenches around me, dragging out the pleasure with each movement.

I growl and pump harder, driving myself even deeper into her. She cries out her release and shudders under me, her pussy tugging on my cock. I suck in a deep breath and shift, adjusting the angle until the head of my cock is dragging along the walls of her pussy at just the right angle to drag me over the edge.

My roar of release echoes in the room as I come, spilling myself into her in hot spurts. I collapse down on her, burying my face into the side of her neck and inhaling her heady scent.

"Holy shit, Andy. That was..."

She chuckles under me, the sound vibrating through her chest and into mine. I push myself up onto my palms and hover over her. The smile pulling on her lips makes my cock twitch inside her.

This woman has managed to work her way inside my heart without me even realizing it. In the short time we've spent together, she's taught me that taking life by the horns and riding it out is the only way to really live.

I kiss her gently, letting my lips linger against hers. She weaves her fingers through my hair and responds in kind, tangling her tongue with mine. When we finally come back up for air, I push back and pull out of her.

We both groan at the loss of contact. She shifts up onto her elbows and I shove away from the table to give her room to stand. The movement sends a box tumbling off the edge of the table and several large bones fall out onto the linoleum floor.

"Shit." I hope nothing broke. That's one of the boxes I moved out of the way earlier and meant to put back onto one of the shelves to examine later. The box simply says "uncategorized bones" and lists a location and date from a dig in the Black Hills.

I reach down and tug up my pants, then I move over and bend down to examine the bones for any damage.

"What the hell?"

These aren't from any species I've ever seen before.

"What's wrong? Did they break?" Andy kneels down next to me.

I shake my head and hold the partial femur up for her to see. "No, but I think you just helped me discover a new species."

"You're kidding."

I turn my head and grin at her. "Nope. I've never seen anything like this before. We're going to be famous."

She laughs and pats me on the shoulder before rising to her feet. "You mean you're going to be famous."

I rise and shake my head. "No, *we* are, because I'm going to name it after you."

She presses her palm to my chest and grins at me. "Well, Dr. Boner, I have to say, I'm pretty impressed with your skills."

"Are you ever going to stop calling me Dr. Boner?"

Her laughter fills the room, and she shakes her head. "Unlikely."

I grin and tug her tightly against me. "I can live with that."

EPILOGUE

One Year Later

"And that's why the avian dinosaurs, the ones that could fly, managed to survive while the rest went extinct at the end of the Cretaceous Period and the beginning of the Paleogene." Rafe sets the bone he's holding on the table in front of him and smiles at the camera. "That's all the time we have for today. Thanks so much for joining me."

The director climbs from his chair and waves to the cameramen to stop filming.

"Cut! That's a wrap!"

Rafe's attention shifts from the camera to me, and he gives me a sly smile that tells me he's already planning all sorts of debauchery for when we're finally alone. I shift in my heels to try to quell the dull throb between my legs that just that look manages to create.

Down, girl.

It's been a hell of a week, and, between Rafe filming and my job, we've barely seen each other.

Nothing will be better than crawling under the covers with him. Or maybe being pinned against a wall. Or smashed awkwardly into the backseat of his car...

There are so many possibilities.

And they all sound amazing right now.

We can finally enjoy ourselves and relax now that things have returned to normal.

Rafe was right. Hollywood forgets things fast. A new scandal always takes the place of the old, and within six months, no one gave a shit about what happened between me and Rafe or the wardrobe malfunction.

Sure, every once in a while, something pops up online mentioning his dickslip or calling him The Boner Doctor, but for the most part, everyone moved on to something more salacious.

And Rafe was way too good on camera to be forgotten and tossed aside for too long. Webflix came looking for him and offered him an enormous contract for a series on their streaming service. He leapt at the chance to get back in front of the camera even though he still continues his work with the museum. Discovering the new species reignited his interest in dig work, and before we know it, he'll be off halfway around the world looking for something else new and undiscovered that he can film for the series.

But not for a while.

For now, he's all mine.

Rafe finishes talking with one of the production staff, and his eyes meet mine again. He slips around the table on set and makes his way over to where I stand waiting.

"Hey, beautiful. I didn't expect to see you here today." His arm slides around my lower back, and he tugs me against his firm body to plant a kiss on my lips. When our mouths meet, a little shock of electricity travels down my spine. Even after all this time, this man still does that to me.

His tongue slips along my lips, urging me to open for him, but I pull away, conscious that we have a rather large audience running around.

"I wanted to surprise you. My meeting ended early, so I headed over."

I couldn't spend another afternoon in the office. It's not that I don't love my job. I'm frankly happy I was even able to get hired again after the scandal. Spending my afternoon dealing with mind-numbing telephone calls and in arguments with producers about budgets for projects was just not going to happen today. I needed a break. I needed Rafe.

Now that I'm in his arms, all the stress of being a CEO of a new, up and coming network dissipates instantly. He always does this to me, makes everything else in the world disappear the moment he touches me. He is my escape, my life, my entire world, and I'm his.

I lean up on my tip-toes and press my lips to his ear. "Can you get out of here?"

His body presses into mine, and his very large, straining cock nudges my stomach. What I wouldn't give to drop to my knees and worship him right now…

Rafe smiles and gives me a little half-pout. "Baby, I would love nothing more than to sneak away with you right now. But I do need to take care of something quickly first. Give me five minutes, tops."

I drop back to my feet and raise an eyebrow. "Five minutes. Then I am hunting your ass down and dragging you out of here."

A smile tugs at the corners of his mouth. "Understood, ma'am." He winks, reaches down and adjusts his cock behind his zipper, then takes off across the sound stage toward a group of production crew congregated in the corner.

He pulls someone aside, and I have to cover my grin with my hand when I recognize Munro.

Karma finally caught up with that dirty fucker. Seeing him working for Rafe gives me way more satisfaction than it should. But we all know he was the one behind our relationship being leaked. His show being cancelled was just him getting what was coming to him, and when he came begging to Rafe for a job on his new show, I knew Rafe would hire him even with the bad history. That's just how Rafe is. A genuinely good guy who wouldn't wish anything bad on anyone.

I can't say I'm so blasé about the whole situation. If Munro had come crawling to me in the same situation, I would have milked that shit and turned him into my personal slave.

Rafe claps Munro on the back and makes his way back toward me.

My eyes drift to his crotch. The thing that brought us together in the first place.

He's managed to contain that raging erection he had, but when I drag my attention back up to his face, the smirk there says he caught me staring. Knowing him, it will probably mean another hard-on before he even makes it all the way over to me.

"What were you looking at?" He stops in front of me and raises an eyebrow.

I don't bother to hide it this time when I look down at his crotch.

"Just what's mine."

He barks out a laugh and leans in to kiss me gently. "Yes, it is yours. Now let's get out of here so you can have your way with it."

If you enjoyed *Dickslip (A Scandalous Slip Story #1)*, make sure to check out *Nipslip (A Scandalous Slip Story #2) and Beaver Blunder (A Scandalous Slip Story #3)*.
Dickslip – www.book2read.com/Dickslip
Nipslip – www.books2read.com/Nipslip
Beaver Blunder - www.books2read.com/BeaverBlunder
To stay connected about new releases and other news, join Gwyn's newsletter here:
www.gwynmcnamee.com/newsletter

ABOUT THE AUTHOR

Gwyn McNamee is an attorney, writer, wife, and mother (to one human baby and two fur babies). Originally from the Midwest, Gwyn relocated to her husband's home town of Las Vegas in 2015 and is enjoying her respite from the cold and snow. Gwyn has been writing down her crazy stories and ideas for years and finally decided to share them with the world. She loves to write stories with a bit of suspense and action mingled with romance and heat. When she isn't either writing or voraciously devouring any books she can get her hands on, Gwyn is busy adding to her tattoo collection, golfing, and stirring up trouble with her perfect mix of sweetness and sarcasm (usually while wearing heels). An admitted shoe whore, Gwyn's closet rivals Carrie Bradshaw's and is constantly expanding.

Gwyn loves to hear from her readers. Here is where you can find her:

Website: https://www.gwynmcnamee.com

Facebook: https://www.facebook.com/AuthorGwynMcNamee/

FB Reader Group: https://www.facebook.com/groups/1667380963540655/

Twitter: https://twitter.com/GwynMcNamee

Instagram: https://www.instagram.com/gwynmcnamee

Bookbub: https://www.bookbub.com/authors/gwyn-mcnamee

OTHER WORKS BY GWYN MCNAMEE

The Slip Series

Dickslip (A Scandalous Slip Story #1)

One wardrobe malfunction. Two lives forever changed.
Playing in a star-studded charity basketball game should be fun, and it is, until I literally go balls out to show up my arch nemesis. When I dive for the basketball and my junk slips out of my gym shorts, I know my life and career are over. There's no way the network can keep my kids' show on the air after I've exposed myself to millions of people. I don't know how Andy, the new CEO, can go to bat for me with such passion. I also never anticipate how hot she looks in a pair of high heels.

Rafe's dickslip has made my new job even more stressful. It's hard enough being a woman in a man's world without dealing with sex organs being publicly displayed when someone is representing the company. But he's an asset to the network, not to mention hot as hell. I can barely keep my eyes off him or his crotch during our meetings. Defending him to the board puts my ass on the line as much as his, but it's worth it. So is risking my job to fulfill the fantasies I've had about him since he first set foot in my office.

Things may have started out bad, but...

Some accidents have happy endings.

Books2read.com/Dickslip

Nipslip (A Scandalous Slip Story #2)

One nipple. A world of problems.

I own the runway. Until my nipple pops out of my dress during New York Fashion Week and it suddenly owns me. Being called a worthless gutter slut by a fuming designer is the least of my problems. My career is swirling around the toilet like the other models' lunches. Until smoking hot Tate Decker steps in with a crazy idea about how his magazine can maybe salvage my livelihood.

It's less than two feet in front of me. Perfect and perky and pink. And the woman it's attached to looks absolutely horrified. I need to help her, and not just because she's beautiful and has a perfect rack. Using my position in the industry to expose the volatile nature of our business puts my career in jeopardy in an attempt to save Riley's. I'm willing to risk that, but falling for her isn't part of the plan.

When love and tits are involved...

Things can get slippery.

Books2read.com/Nipslip

Beaver Blunder (A Scandalous Slip Story #3)

One brief mistake. A world of hurt.

No panties. No problem. At least until I slip on the wet floor and go heels over head in front of my colleagues and half the courthouse. Returning to consciousness can't be more awkward, until I find out who my sexy, argumentative, and bossy knight in shining armor really is. My career may not survive my beaver blunder, and my heart might not survive Owen Grant.

Madeline Ryan tumbles into my life on a wave of perfume and public embarrassment. She falls and exposes herself in front of me, and I find myself falling for her despite the fact she fights me every chance she gets. Being a woman in a good ol' boy profession demands a certain brashness, but it definitely has me thinking, maybe litigators shouldn't be lovers.

With stressful jobs and big attitudes, going commando has never been so freeing.

Books2read.com/BeaverBlunder

The Hawke Family Series
Savage Collision (The Hawke Family - Book One)

The last thing I expect when I walk into The Hawkeye Club is to fall head over heels in lust. It's supposed to be a rescue mission. I have to get my baby sister off the pole, into some clothes, and out of the grasp of the pussy peddler who somehow manipulated her into stripping. But the moment I see Savage Hawke and verbally spar with him, my ability to remain rational flies out the window and my libido takes center stage. I've never wanted a relationship—my time is better spent focusing on taking down the scum running this city—but what I want and what I need are apparently two different things.

Danika Eriksson storms into my office in her high heels and on her high horse. Her holier-than-thou attitude and accusations should offend me, but instead, I can't get her out of my head or my heart. Her incomparable drive, take-no-prisoners attitude, and blatant honesty captivate me and hold me prisoner. I should steer clear, but my self-preservation instinct is apparently dead—which is exactly what our relationship will be once she knows everything. It's only a matter of time.

The truth doesn't always set you free. Sometimes, it just royally screws you.

AVAILABLE NOW: https://www.books2read.com/u/mYR1gY

Tortured Skye (The Hawke Family - Book Two)

Falling in love with Gabe Anderson was as easy as breathing. Fighting my feelings for my brother's best friend was agonizingly hard. I never imagined giving in to my desire for him would cause such a destructive ripple effect. That kiss was my grasp at a lifeline—something, anything to hold me steady in my crumbling life. Now, I have to suffer with the fallout while trying to convince him it's all worth the consequences.

Guilt overwhelms me—over what I've done, the lives I've taken, and more than anything, over my feelings for Skye Hawke. Craving my best friend's little sister is insanely self-destructive. It never should have happened, but since the moment she kissed me, I haven't been able to get her out of my mind. If I take what I want, I risk losing everything. If I don't, I'll lose her and a piece of myself. The raging storm threatening to rain down on the city is nothing compared to the one that will come from my decision.

Love can be torture, but sometimes, love is the only thing that can save you.

AVAILABLE NOW: https://www.books2read.com/u/mdK2RX

Stone Sober (The Hawke Family - Book Three)

Stone Hawke is precisely the kind of man women are warned about— handsome, intelligent, arrogant, and intricately entangled with some dangerous people. I should stay away, but he manages to strip my soul bare with just a look and dominates my thoughts. Bad decisions are in my past. My life is (mostly) on track, even if it is no longer the one to medical school. I can't allow myself to cave to the fierce pull and ardent attraction I feel toward the youngest Hawke.

Nora Eriksson is off-limits, and not just because she's my brother's employee and sister-in-law. Despite the fact she's stripping at The Hawkeye Club, she has an innocent and pure heart. Normally, the only thing that appeals to me about innocence is the opportunity to taint it. But not when it comes to Nora. I can't expose her to the filth permeating my life. There are too many things I can't control, things completely out of my hands. She doesn't deserve any of it, but the power she holds over me is stronger than any addiction.

The hardest battles we fight are often with ourselves, but only through defeating our own demons can we find true peace.

AVAILABLE NOW:
https://www.books2read.com/u/b6rMGJ

Building Storm (The Hawke Family - Book Four)
COMING 2018

Continue reading for a sneak peek at *Savage Collision*

SAVAGE COLLISION (THE HAWKE FAMILY – BOOK ONE) EXCERPT

Naked women gyrate on stages—asses, tits, flesh on display—their images covering three-quarters of my computer screen, but they are merely blurs in my peripheral vision.

My focus is on the top right corner, where one of my vendors is unloading his truck on the loading dock, and taking his sweet-ass time doing it. He's no doubt using it as an excuse to gawk at the girls. Byron, my club manager, is in heated discussion with him about something. Hopefully, he's reaming him out for taking up so much of our damn time with an unload that should take only minutes.

Why are people so fucking lazy these days? What happened to work ethic?

My parents made damn well sure all their children understood the importance of a hard-day's work and always giving it one hundred percent. I guess that kind of thing just isn't instilled in people anymore. It shouldn't surprise me really, the degradation of society, not when I see the degenerates who always manage to find their way in here, despite my best efforts to keep the club clientele upscale.

Byron and the vendor move to the back of the truck and start unloading several handcarts-full of cases of beer at a time. At least I can always rely on Byron to get the job done.

I return to the paperwork on my desk but barely have time to regain my train of thought before my office door flies open, slamming against the wall.

Instinctively, I reach under my desk, wrapping my hand around the grip of the Sig Sauer 1911 Scorpion I keep mounted there. I look up, expecting to find one of Domenico Abello's thugs, because, surely, that would be the only person capable of making it past both Gabe and Byron to end up in my office unannounced.

My breath catches in my throat when, instead of a burly threat, my eyes land on what I can only describe as a Victoria's Secret model. An enraged one.

She is furious—the fire in her stormy blue eyes and her scowling red lips are a dead giveaway. With a toss of her long, wavy blonde hair behind her shoulder, she thunders into my office as if she owns the place.

I track her progress across the room, taking in her polished appearance—from her French-manicured nails, thousand-dollar bag, and Burberry trench down to the four-inch Louboutin stilettos that make her long, elegant legs extend beyond comprehension as she clicks across the wood floor with purpose.

My cock hardens instantly and, despite my surprise at my body's reaction to her, I steel my expression and shift uncomfortably in my chair.

Damn. This woman is livid, and hot as fucking hell.

I doubt she's a threat, though—to anything but my libido—so, I remove my hand from the gun and surreptitiously slide it to my crotch to adjust my erection before reclining and watching her speculatively. Despite this being my office, my domain, I wait patiently for her to say something. I see a hint of uncertainty and maybe discomfort beneath her diamond-hard demeanor.

"Are you the owner?"

She stops several feet short of my desk, props her hands on her shapely hips and huffs in defiance. Her voice is level and steady when she asks the question, but her eyes give her away. They roam over me with blatant interest and the slight flush on her neck and cheeks only confirm my suspicion—she's checking me out.

I relax in my chair and school my features, trying to hide my amusement. I answer her question with a nod. "I am, and you might be?"

"Danika Eriksson." She tosses her name at me like a poison dart, and her bravado impresses me despite my uncertainty about her purpose here.

Do I know her? Should I be recognizing her name? No, I would remember a woman like her.

Movement in the open door catches my eye and I see Gabe, my best friend, right-hand man, and business partner eyeing Ms. Eriksson with concern. I wave him off with a look and he nods his understanding before disappearing down the hall. "What can I do for you, Ms. Eriksson?"

She crosses her arms over her chest in a huff, which only succeeds in pushing her abundant breasts higher on her chest.

Not helping the raging hard-on situation, lady.

"You can tell me where the hell you get off tricking young, innocent girls into selling themselves like slabs of beef in your disgusting club." She spits the words at me, completely, unabashedly unafraid to insult me and my business, while standing right in front of me and looking me in the eye.

I struggle to withhold a grin at her audacity as I lean forward, resting my elbows on the edge of the desk.

"I can assure you, Ms. Eriksson, that none of my employees are 'tricked' into doing anything."

She scoffs and shifts her weight, drawing my attention back to her impossibly long, shapely legs. The woman must be at least five foot seven without those heels on. With them, she towers over me in all her elegant glory.

"Bullshit..." She searches my desk for a nameplate, then looks at me again when she doesn't find one.

The corner of my mouth quirks up before I can stop it. "Savage, Savage Hawke. But please, call me Savage, and just what is it you think you know about my employees?"

"Savage?" Her eyes narrow and then she rolls them. "Your parents honestly named you Savage Hawke?"

This isn't the first time someone has questioned my name, or that my name has left me the butt of some joke. "Yes, they did. It's a family name." My gaze naturally drifts to the framed photo on the corner of my desk. It was my father's second-to-last fight. He's standing in the center of the ring in Madison Square Garden, the WBA heavy-weight championship belt around his waist, and I'm hoisted above his head, both of us smiling in his victory. I was ten.

She follows my stare and when she sees the photo, her eyebrows pop up in recognition. "Wait, your father is Sam 'The Savage' Hawke?"

Stunned doesn't even begin to describe how I feel, hearing my dad's name from her. It takes me a moment to shake off my surprise, but eventually, I manage a smile and nod. "I'm surprised you recognize him." I lean forward to grab the photo and turn it around so she can see it more clearly.

In my thirty years on this planet, I don't think I've ever

met a single woman who knew who my father was. Men, on the other hand, gape in awe when they find out my lineage. I guess it just goes with the territory of being the son of a heavy-weight champ, and one who died the way he did.

She takes a step closer to me, bending down slightly to get closer look at the photo. "Holy shit! I can't believe you are 'The Savage's' son! Of course I know who he is. My dad was a huge boxing fan. I grew up watching your dad's fights from my old man's lap."

"That's great." And very unexpected. I'm not quite sure what to say. Talking about my father is always bittersweet.

Her smile and astonishment fade and she glances at me apologetically. "Shit, I'm sorry..." Before she finishes her thought, she seems to realize she's been sidetracked from her intended purpose. She straightens herself, squares her shoulders, and I can tell she's ready to get back to business.

"Well, Savage," she says my name like it's a four-letter word, "I would very much appreciate it if you kept your sleazy hands off my baby sister."

Bingo!

She isn't the first, and she certainly won't be the last, person to find their way into my office on their high horse, accusing me of taking advantage of some innocent little sister, cousin, or friend.

"And who is your baby sister?"

Her face scrunches in disgust at my inability to immediately make the familial connection.

"Nora Eriksson, she started shaking her ass and tits for you almost three weeks ago."

The way she throws the words "ass and tits" at me, I have to cover my mouth with my hand to hide my grin. This woman is all attitude and it is sexy as fuck, although I have no idea why. She definitely isn't my usual type, although, I'm not sure if I even know what my type is anymore. Certainly, she's about as far from Becca as one can get, yet my cock is still straining against my pants.

I clear my throat before responding, hoping to give myself a second to regain my composure. "Ah, yes, Nora. My manager, Byron, hired her. I've only had the pleasure of meeting her on one occasion, but I can assure you, Ms. Eriksson, she was in no way 'tricked' into taking her position here."

She glowers at me and her hands ball into tight fists at her sides. "I know my sister, *Savage*, and there is no way in hell she just up and decided she wanted to be a fucking stripper. She was tricked, or forced…"

I barely manage to contain an eye-roll. "If I didn't have such thick skin, I might be insulted by the way you throw your words at me like daggers," I retort, enjoying watching her distress at my ability to maintain my cool. The color in her cheeks flares and her blue eyes flash at me.

Who knew angry could be such a fucking turn on?

My blood is boiling and this man—Savage Hawke—has grated my last nerve. I can barely contain my desire to climb across his desk and smack him across his handsome, smug face for acting so high and mighty. He is a pussy peddler. A goddamn sleazebag who preys on young, impressionable, desperate girls in order to make a quick buck.

Savage Hawke.

He even has a porn star name. It wouldn't surprise me if he was shooting them in some back room.

It's too bad he's so fucking gorgeous. He runs a hand back through his thick, wavy black hair and focuses his Caribbean-blue eyes on me with a calm that makes me want to throw my purse at him.

My traitorous body reacted to him instantly, heat churning deep in my belly the moment I walked into his office and saw him dominating the space behind his large, wooden desk.

The longer we talk, the worse it gets, and I have to press my thighs together to stop the dull ache there.

Damn, it has been way too long since I had a good fuck. What? Twelve days?

I'm so busy fuming and trying to rein in my runaway sex drive, I completely forget to respond to him.

"Ms. Eriksson," he continues, giving me a smug smile, "I have a very rigorous interview process established to ensure none of my employees begin work here under any duress..."

I lift my brow in speculation and to ensure he's aware of my disbelief. *Bullshit!* I bet their "interview process" involves lap dances and blowjobs in the champagne room.

"...Byron conducts a very thorough interview with each girl, including a complete background check to determine if they are under any serious financial strains. If I find they are, I typically offer them a personal loan, to be repaid at standard interest rates, to ensure they aren't tempted to engage in pursuits some of the other clubs are often known for. We also do weekly drug testing and nightly breathalyzers, as our girls are forbidden from engaging in any illicit drug use and cannot perform while under the influence of any alcoholic beverages."

I don't believe him for a second. No damn strip club operates like that. He must think I'm some dumb, naïve, bimbo blonde to think I'll fall for his line of horseshit.

He reclines back in his chair and waits for me to say something.

What does he expect me to believe? That he's a pussy peddler with a heart of gold?

"Surprised I'm not a total scumbag?" His amusement is evident in the slight turn at the corner of his luscious mouth. "There are a hundred trashy strip clubs in New Orleans a man can go to if that's what he's looking for—drugs and easy women. I wanted to offer something different. People are always a bit shocked to learn how I run my business. But when I built The Hawkeye Club, I wanted it to be an upscale and supremely classy gentleman's club, and established a very strict set of rules and regulations to ensure that both my reputation, and the reputation of my girls, remains pristine."

I huff and take a step closer to his desk. "My sister was the goddamn valedictorian of her high school class and had a full ride to Tulane for pre-med. Then, this morning, out of the blue, I find out from one of her roommates that she has dropped out of school and started working here. She's twenty years old, for Christ's sake! Clearly, you can see why I'm concerned. I mean, why the hell would she do that?"

He offers me a small, understanding smile and leans over his desk, toward me. The fabric of his dress shirt stretches across his broad shoulders and strains against his massive biceps. My mouth salivates and I fight the flush I'm sure is creeping up my neck. The worst thing about being fair-skinned is the complete inability to hide my reactions, especially to men like Savage Hawke.

"I do understand, Ms. Eriksson, but I don't have the answer for you. Have you tried asking your sister?"

Shit. I should have seen that question coming.

I shift uncomfortably and twist my hands in front of my body. "No, she's been avoiding my calls. That's why I finally went to her apartment today, to make sure she's okay."

He almost looks sympathetic and I wonder how long it took him to perfect this nice-guy act.

"Well, I think you need to talk to her. I don't think she's on the schedule tonight, but you can ask Byron downstairs, and, if she's here, he will gladly show you to the changing rooms in the back so you can speak with her."

Casting an uncomfortable glance toward him, I move my purse from one shoulder to the other and turn to leave without a word. Absolutely no good will come from me spending any more time in this room with this man.

Savage Hawke is precisely the type of man I always end up getting myself into trouble with: dark, strong, passionate...

I almost stumble when a vision of him slamming me back against the wall and yanking up my skirt to gain access floods my mind.

Jesus—I bet he takes absolute control in the bedroom, and I bet he fucks like a complete animal. Men like that don't do things slow and sweet.

"I don't even get a 'thank you' or a 'goodbye?'"

His sultry, deep voice stops me halfway to the door. I look over my shoulder at him.

Deep breaths, Dani. Keep it together.

Don't let him see how he affects you. Don't let him see you rattled.

"I don't have anything to thank you for," I reply, before raising my head high and strutting out the door, not bothering to close it behind me. I punch the button on the elevator and tap my foot impatiently.

I need to get out of here.

I need to get as far away as possible.

I need to find Nora.

I need to find something to prevent me from racing home, grabbing my Rabbit, and spending the rest of the day fantasizing about that man.

I need to find something to prevent me from racing straight back to his office, climbing over his desk, and straddling his lap.

An angry fuck can be supremely hot—ripped clothing, hair pulling, strong, groping hands—but having an angry fuck with my stripper sister's deviant boss would be an epically bad life choice.

Grab *Savage Collision* at all retailers now!
https://www.books2read.com/u/mYR1gY

Made in the USA
Middletown, DE
15 May 2021